HEART STOPPING

BEST SERVED COLD
BOOK 1

MAGGIE ALABASTER

TRIGGER WARNINGS

Murder

Cannibalism

Torture

Mutilation

Kidnapping

Mentions of child SA, not detailed, never on the page

Mentions of trafficking, not detailed, never on the page

Mentions of drowning, not detailed, never on the page

CHAPTER 1

HARLOW

"Do you have a key?" I asked between frantic kisses.

"Of *course* I have a key. I live here, don't I?" He went to pat his jeans' pocket, to realize they dragged behind him, only his right ankle still encased in denim. He tried to kick it off, but the hem was caught on his shoe.

"Fucking hell." He pressed his palm to the wall beside him, leaned on his arm and yanked off his pants. His shoe came off inside the leg. Triumphant, he snatched his jeans up and rifled through the pockets for his key. Dressed in only a black button down shirt, one shoe, one sock and boxers covered in cartoon birds, he slid the key into the lock and pushed the door open.

He threw his pants inside and gestured for me to follow. "Milady…" He cocked his head expectantly.

His English accent was attractive, but not enough for me to offer my name. Instead, I stepped past him, into his tiny apartment. I barely started to take a look around before he closed the door and pushed me up against it.

"Now, where were we?" He slipped his hands up the front of my shirt and cupped my breasts. His mouth found mine again, his tongue sliding over my lips and pressing inside.

I kissed him back, his light stubble tickling my cheeks.

How long had it been since I had a good fuck? Too long. I didn't usually pick up strays, but for a muscular guy with tousled blonde hair and ridiculously blue eyes, I'd make an exception. It was a fuck, no strings. No fuss. We both understood that.

I pushed his buttons through their holes before working his shirt off his shoulders and letting it drop to the floor. His body was a study in lines, grooves and black ink, complemented by scars that crisscrossed his torso.

"Like what you see?"

I hadn't realized I was staring, but now he was looking at me, satisfied smirk on his face. A dimple popped in one cheek.

"I've seen worse." I trailed my fingers down from his collarbone, over his chest and flat stomach.

He smirked bigger and pushed my shirt up and over my head. "Such a pretty girl." He reached around to flick open the hooks of my bra like he'd done it a million times before.

Cool air hit my nipples, making them harden. Or maybe it was the way he was admiring me, like I was the work of art.

Giving him a speculative look, I hooked my thumbs into the waistband of his boxers and pushed them down his hips. I have to admit, his cock was impressive, long and thick. He was already hard, pre-cum shining as if trying to compete with the piercing on his tip.

"You've had a good look, now it's only fair I return the favor." He pushed my panties down, letting them fall to my ankles. They'd barely touched the floor when he was picking me up and wrapping my legs around his waist. My back against the door, he stroked my clit with his long fingers and pushed the tip of his cock inside my pussy.

My arms around his neck, I held on while pushing him deeper into me, my heels on his firm ass.

"Fuck, girl, you feel like somethin' else," he whispered. He pulled back and thrust in, only to have the door rattle loudly behind us.

A moment later came a pounding on the wall. "Keep it down in there, I'm trying to sleep!"

He muttered something that sounded like, "Fucking tosser," and carried me over to the kitchenette. My ass on the very edge of the counter, he continued fucking and stroking me as though we weren't interrupted at all.

His piercing stroked deep inside me, heightening the pleasure to almost unbearable levels. I bit my lip to keep from screaming. Incredible wasn't enough to describe it.

I was right on the verge of coming when he slid out of me. Ignoring my growl of protest, he lifted me from the counter and lay me down on the couch that took up most of the room. Taking his weight on his knees and elbows, he lay over me and slid back inside me, his thrusts slow.

Between strokes, he licked his way around one of my nipples, then drew it between his lips to suck.

"Has anyone told you you have perfect tits?" he asked, his voice muffled by said tits.

"I might have heard that once or twice before," I said immodestly.

What? They were very good breasts. A girl had to be vain about something; that was mine.

He chuckled. "I'll bet you hear it all the time."

He'd lose that bet, but I didn't mention it. Or much of anything right now. I was occupied with my rapidly rising orgasm. The pressure built like a bomb, set to detonate.

"I'm…going…to…come," I said breathlessly.

I forced one eye open, half expecting him to say he heard that all the time. If he did, he didn't say so. His own eyes were half-closed, concentrating on thrusting, while his hands explored my breasts.

"Let me hear you," was all he said. Then, with a cheeky smile that made his dimple pop again, he said, "Let the neighbors hear."

I had a feeling the walls were so thin the neighbors would hear an ant walking across the floor, much less me having an orgasm. Still, I'd never been quiet and I wasn't going to be quiet now. I tipped back my head and moaned as the tsunami of pleasure washed over me, taking me down from my head to my toes. The whole world disappearing in a haze of stars and bliss, compounded by his own, loud orgasm.

The pounding of blood through my ears was a match for the renewed pounding on the wall. "Shut the fuck up!"

"You can't see me, but I'm flipping you off," he called out loudly before lowering his voice and saying, "Sorry about that arsehole. He needs to get laid. Or I need to find somewhere better to fucking live."

He shrugged, the dimple back in his cheek as he grinned and slid out of me. Before I could say a word, he scooped me up in his arms and carried me to his bedroom.

"Ready for round two?"

————

According to my watch, it was nineteen minutes past two in the morning when I pulled on my clothes, grabbed my shoes, and snuck out of his apartment. To my surprise, there was no complaint from his neighbor about his snoring, which was at least as loud as his moans when he came.

I tucked my shirt into my skirt and crept out, closing the door softly behind me. His shoe, I noticed, was absent from where we left it outside in the hall. Lucky for me I hadn't left mine out there too. I leaned against the wall to push my feet into them and hurried away toward the elevator.

I made it all the way down to the street before anyone witnessed my walk of shame, if you wanted to call it that. The folks who passed me on my two-block walk down the street didn't give me a second look. Of course not, this was New York City, no one cared I fucked a guy I met in a bar. Not even that we had a mere twenty minutes of conversation before heading to his place. Flirting, suggestive comments, then an invitation. From me, to him, but I insisted on going to his place. My apartment was my sanctuary. The place where I could be myself, and keep my secrets intact. My haven.

Half a block down, the sky opened and started to rain. I ducked my head and kept it down until I stepped into my building. Dripping and shivering, I took the elevator up to my floor and let myself in. Closed, locked and bolted the door behind me before slipping the chain into place.

"Did you miss me?" I flicked on the light and look over to my guest.

He blinked against the sudden intrusion of light, and muttered something against the ball gag in his mouth. A muffled plea between drips of water.

A spout in the wall was situated right over the Perspex box he was locked inside. Every thirty seconds or so, it would drip onto a metal plate with a loud plink. The persistent sound wouldn't give him a moment of peace.

Don't feel bad for him. He was trying to sell his stepdaughter to the highest bidder. People, and I use that term loosely, like him didn't deserve mercy.

Did I mention the water was also rising slowly? It slid off the metal plate and plopped into the bottom of the box. Cold and persistent. Right now, it covered his bare hips. Soon, it'd be up to his chin. And then over his face. His wild eyes told me he knew he didn't have long. He still had one thing left though: a shred of hope. That somehow he'd appeal to my humanity and I'd let him out.

Not a chance.

"You still think you're getting out of here alive, don't you Gary?" His name wasn't Gary. It didn't matter what it was. If I called him by his real name, it might humanize him. That wasn't going to happen. He'd surrendered his humanity a long time ago. Sold it off for money, as if it might be worth the price.

I tapped on the side of the box. "You go on thinking that, I need some sleep." I reached over to the tap beside the spout. Noted the look of hope on his face, sure I was about to turn the water off.

Instead, I turned it up, so it was coming out faster, but quieter. There was no point in disturbing my sleep. I had to be up in a couple of hours to get to work.

"Good night, try to get some sleep," I said sweetly. If he managed to lie down, he'd be under the water and we both knew it.

Should I turn the water on all the way and end

him sooner? Having him here alive was a hassle and a risk, but I wanted him to suffer the way he would have let his stepdaughter suffer. Who does that to a twelve-year-old? No, he deserved what he got. The world wouldn't miss him. She certainly wouldn't. With any luck, she'd never know what he had in mind for her. She could keep her innocence for a few more years yet.

He murmured something again, begging, pleading for this to end. It would, soon enough. Until then, he had plenty of time to reflect on what he'd done. He might be a better person in his next life, because he was a shitty person in this one.

I gave him a long look before turning off the light and stepping into my bedroom. This was my sanctuary against the madness. The walls painted a cheerful yellow, the bedspread yellow and blue. If you saw this room and nothing else, you'd never know the depths of darkness in my soul. The things I'd seen and done.

Harlow St. James was no ray of sunshine, in spite of having perfect breasts. I straddled the line between avenging angel and monster. A line so fine, sometimes I couldn't see it, especially with the lights out.

I stripped off and took a quick shower, washing the night's activities from my body. Cleaning up carefully around the delicious ache in my pussy and thighs. He really knew what to do with a girl. Shame I'd never see him again.

I turned off the water and dried myself before pulling on pajamas and slipping under my sheets. The hum of traffic outside soothed me, almost drowning out the drip of water into Gary's box. He shuffled around, trying to get comfortable, or maybe looking for a way out. There wasn't one, not from the inside. Especially not with his wrists bound to his ankles.

No, once the water took him, the only place he was going was straight to Hades.

CHAPTER 2

HARLOW

"That's the last one, chef," Gina called out.

I glanced back over my shoulder and gave her a curt nod. Pushing damp, red hair off my face, I finished stirring the Bolognese sauce and set the lid on top. One of our most popular dishes, I was always making tonight's batch while finishing off the lunch rush. Now, it would sit and simmer for a few hours to increase the depth of flavor.

"That was brutal." My kitchen hand, Erin, bustled around grabbing up empty pots and spoons to wash them.

"Wouldn't have it any other way, would we?" I washed my hands and dried them before shrugging out of my chef jacket.

She grinned. "Nah, keeps things interesting." She

dumped everything into the sink and started to scrub.

She'd been with me for a year now and knew what I expected. Spotless everything. Above and beyond Health Department guidelines. Angel's Rest had been in immaculate shape since I opened it two years ago. No one was going to shut us down. We weren't going to end up on an episode of some show with Gordon Ramsay telling us to pick up our game. No, if he ate here, he'd be singing our praises.

"Yeah, it does," I agreed. I hung my jacket on a hook and stepped out of the kitchen to greet any diners who remained.

A couple sat at the table beside the window, finishing off their chicken Caesar salads. Every so often, he'd say something and she'd laugh. She might not laugh so hard if she knew he was here last week with his wife. And the week before that with a different woman. Which, of course, was none of my business. As long as none of them was underage, I'd turn a blind eye.

If they were underage, he'd be dealt with.

A guy sat alone at another table, dark hair hanging over his glasses. He absently shoved it off his face. Immediately, it fell right back down. He didn't seem to notice. His attention was on the tablet in front of him, occasionally picking up his milkshake to take a sip.

Heavy on the chocolate, they were another favorite with customers.

Placing the straw between his lips, he went to suck, the glass was empty. He stared at it like emptied itself, before putting it back on the table and pushing his hair back again.

I made my way over to pick up the glass, since Gina was busy clearing another table. As soon as I got close enough, he turned off the screen and looked up at me. Not like he had something to hide, but rather that he was giving me all his attention.

"Hey." He pushed his glasses back up his nose.

"Hey," I said with equal eloquence. He was cute, in a nerdy sort of way. Like a hot computer programmer. One who probably lived in his parents' basement, only leaving once in a while to have a milkshake.

"You're the chef here, right?" he asked.

"Chef and owner," I confirmed.

"You make a good milkshake," he said. "I'm Cassius." Looking chagrined he added, "Titmus." He held out his hand.

I looked at it for a moment before offering a fist bump instead of a shake. If there was something I hated, it was shaking hands with people.

He rallied quickly, curling his hand into a fist to bump before dropping it back to the table. "Sorry, social norms are not my strong point." As if the faded *X-Files* T-shirt wasn't a clear indication of that.

I shrugged one shoulder. "Mine either. Food makes more sense to me than people."

He grinned, showing a couple of slightly crooked teeth, but a warm smile. "Relatable. People never make sense to me." For a moment, his expression darkened, but lifted again like a stiff breeze blew a cloud away from in front of the sun. "Milkshakes are easier."

"Milkshakes don't tend to have expectations," I agreed. "They just…are."

"Especially yours," he said. "Secret ingredient?"

"Of course, but it's called *secret* for a reason." I was starting to wonder if he was a journalist, or worked for a rival restaurant. If that was the case, he was out of luck. He wouldn't get any secrets from me.

"As long as it's not made with any human bodily fluids," he said.

"No, that's the salted caramel," I deadpanned. "The salt has to come from somewhere." I flashed him a smile before heading to the kitchen to hand the empty glass to Erin.

"What did you say to him?" She was peering out of the kitchen in Cassius' direction. "I can't tell if he's turned on or scared out of his wits. I wouldn't rule out both."

I glanced over my shoulder. Sure enough, he was staring at me, his plush lips parted. His hair fell all the way over one lens, but he didn't seem to have noticed.

"I don't think you're supposed to traumatize customers," she teased.

"No, that's my job." Gina bounced into the kitchen, arms laden with plates. "I don't think it's worked with him. He's been in here every day this week. He's ordered every different flavor of milkshake. Never has anything else."

I narrowed my eyes at him, causing him to look away, his cheeks slightly red. "Has he been asking what we put in the milkshakes?"

Gina cocked her head before shaking it. "No, he just orders one and sits there looking at his tablet. He seemed harmless enough to me." She grabbed up a washcloth and headed out to wipe down the tables while Erin did the last of the dishes.

"Harmless enough, huh?" I muttered to myself. Yeah, people thought Gary was 'harmless enough' until he tried to make money by nefarious means.

Honestly, I wanted to believe Cassius Titmus was harmless, but there was something about him. A layer of darkness underneath the milkshake-sipping geek. Maybe he burnt ants with a magnifying glass for fun.

I stepped over to work on tweaking next week's menu. When I turned back, he was gone, along with the other couple. Gina was closing and locking the door behind them and turning the sign to closed. In a few hours, we'd be back for the dinner rush, but in the meantime, we'd take a break.

I shooed both women out the back door before closing and locking it behind us. Giggling about something, they headed off down the street, leaving me to step the other way. I almost ran straight into Cassius.

I startled and staggered a couple of steps back. Almost tripped on a crack in the sidewalk and fell on my ass. At the last moment, I threw out a hand to the wall beside me, keeping myself from falling.

"Sorry, didn't mean to scare you," he said. He raised his hand in a gesture of placation.

"You didn't. I didn't see you there, that's all," I said, pushing away from the wall. "Do you always lurk around in alleys waiting for women to step out?"

He offered a lopsided smile. "Not always, only once in a while. And only when the woman is beautiful." His gaze dropped to my lips for a moment before returning to my eyes. "And makes a mean milkshake."

"Still not giving you the secret ingredient." I started to step past him.

"I'm not asking," he said quickly. "I saw you in there the other day and I've been trying to get up the nerve to talk to you. Like I said, social norms aren't my strong suit. Some people would describe me as awkward as fuck."

"Fuck is pretty awkward," I said.

"I think I exceed it," he admitted.

"Right; I should go," I said.

"Wait can I ask you—" He put a hand out toward me.

Without thinking, I grabbed his wrist, dropped my upper body and threw him over my shoulder and onto the ground. He landed with a thud, bounced once before lying still, staring up at me. His tablet flew out of his hand and skittered a couple of feet away.

"Okay, that was hot." He blinked a few times before he moved and winced.

"Shit." I fixed my messy bun and stepped away from him. Throwing wasn't supposed to be hot. It was a reflex. A response to a perceived threat.

Seeing him lying there like that, I wanted to kick myself. He didn't look like a threat right then.

He looked like a lawsuit waiting to happen.

"I'm sorry," I started to say.

Fuck. Fuckfuckfuck. I always knew my paranoia would get the better of me someday, but I didn't expect it to be like this. Out in the street where anyone could have seen me in action.

He scrambled to his feet, his hands raised again. "No, I'm sorry. You must think I'm a total idiot. Hell, I think I'm a total idiot." He knitted his heavy brows. "I just wanted to ask you to dinner, but I get it. I've never been good at making first impressions." He sighed heavily.

"It's not you," I assured him. "You seem nice. I'm just not very…trusting."

That was putting it lightly.

I snatched up his tablet and handed it to him. Thank all the gods it didn't seem to be damaged.

"Come back for lunch tomorrow and I'll give you all the milkshakes you can handle." Yes, I wasn't above bribing him so he didn't sue my ass into the ground. If I had to give him free milkshakes for the rest of my life, and that's what I'd do.

It was a small price to pay when you thought about it. None of this had anything to do with wanting to see him again. Or so I told myself.

"I can handle a lot of milkshakes." He held his tablet against his chest and smiled. "Can we, I don't know, be friends? I… I don't even know your name." He held out his fist again for another bump, his body tense as if expecting to find himself on the concrete again.

"Harlow." I swiped my fist over his. "I don't think you want me for a friend."

Unless he just wanted me for my milkshakes. I'd say he was the first, but he wasn't. What can I say, food has an interesting effect on people. Especially when they stood to make money from it. I got at least one visit a month from someone working with my rivals, trying to learn something to give them an advantage.

Lucky for me, my staff was loyal. That's what I got for paying above minimum wage. And giving them time off when they need it. None of them would risk losing their job. Besides, we were a close-knit group of people, even if they didn't know about my…extracurricular activities.

"I really do," he said earnestly. "Maybe you can teach me how to throw people."

He mimed grabbing someone and throwing them over his shoulder. Then clasped his hands in front of himself and raised them, tablet and all, over his hand like he'd won a wrestling match. If the match was geek versus geek.

I found myself smiling. "I'll think about it. I should get going; I have things to do before the dinner rush."

"Of course." He lowered his hands again. "Me too. I'll see you tomorrow." He started to back away, jumped as he bumped into a dumpster and jerked away, laughing at himself.

I shook my head at him and watched him turn and hurry off down the street. I had to admit he had a very grabable ass, even in his faded jeans.

"Cass," I called out after him without thinking.

He stopped and turned around, a questioning look on his face. "Yeah?"

"Does anyone call you that?" I asked.

He shrugged and smiled. "They do now." He gave me a salute before he turned away again and disappeared amongst the crowds on the sidewalk.

"Bye," I said under my breath. If Cass knew what was good for him, he'd stay far away from me.

With a sigh, I headed off to my apartment to check on Gary. I sensed he was close to cracking and giving me the names of the people he was working with. If he did, I might let him die sooner.

CHAPTER 3

HARLOW

"Are you sure this is the place, Gary?" I was talking to myself because Gary was back at my place, with water up to his chin. He'd been forthcoming about some of the people in his operation, but not enough to save his own ass.

Let's face it, his ass was wrinkled toast a long time ago.

I checked the address again before silently making my way up the fire escape like a shadow. All the way up to the sixth floor. Stepping carefully past a couple of half open windows until I reached one in semi-darkness.

I crouched in front of it, peering through a gap in the curtain. A figure paced past, then back again. I froze when he spoke. Let out a silent breathe when I realized he was talking on the phone.

"It doesn't matter, Frank, I need to know where…"
He paced away again.

If he was looking for Gary, he was shit out of luck. On the other hand, they'd meet again soon enough.

I sensed something was off a moment before I heard the creak of the fire escape below me.

Fuck.

They were moving almost as quietly as I had, but the metal wasn't as forgiving under their weight as it was under mine.

I peered downward. Someone was making their way up toward me, freezing every time the stairs groaned.

Double fuck.

The only way out of here was into the building or back down the way I'd come. If they came all the way up here, they wouldn't miss seeing me.

They started up again, fourth floor, fifth.

I silently pulled out a knife and waited. If they thought I'd be easy pickings, they were mistaken. I was ready to—

"What the hell?" I whispered. I knew that stubbled face, the blonde hair. The sounds he made when he came.

The dimple as he grinned and whispered back, "Hello, love. I almost didn't recognize you with your clothes on. Didn't expect to find you in a place like this."

"What are you doing here?" I whispered. "You can't be here." I held the knife against my hip, where he couldn't see it. Obscured by the curve of my ass.

"I was going to say the same to you." He looked past me toward the window. "Friend of yours?"

"No," I said quickly. What the ever-loving fuck was going on right now? "Why are you here?"

"I could sell you a bunch of bullshit," he said in his all-too-attractive English accent, "but since you're crouched out here too, I figure we might be here for the same reason."

"Interesting theory," I said slowly. "You tell me yours first." I reminded my clit sleeping with him the other night was a one time thing. We weren't going to fuck, on this fire escape. For so many reasons.

"I don't believe we've been officially introduced," he said. "My name is Edward Bonegard, but you can call me Boner."

"I'm not calling you Boner," I said, a little more scathing than I intended.

He lowered himself down beside me and crossed his legs. "Suit yourself, love, but that's what everyone calls me."

"By everyone, do you mean you and your reflection?" I asked.

He chuckled. "You should give me more credit. You've seen the evidence. I seem to remember fucking you with it a couple of nights ago. You weren't complaining."

"That was then. You still haven't told me why you're here." If he was trying to get me to let down my guard, he was going to have to work harder than that. Sex was one thing, revealing my secrets was another.

Boner, I guess I was calling him that after all, nodded toward the window.

"That man, and I use that term loosely, inside that apartment likes to assault young girls," he said, not pulling any punches now. "I thoroughly object to him, or anyone else, doing so. With all that in mind, I came to stop him from touching any other girls ever again. As, I think, did you."

"Do I look like someone who'd kill a total stranger?" I asked, trying to sound offended. Pretending he hadn't hit the nail right on the head.

"How do I put this?" he said slowly. "You look like the sort of woman who'd be very good at taking care of herself. And others. Sometimes that calls for... extreme measures."

I looked away, towards the street. I hadn't always managed to take care of the people I cared about. That was a shortcoming of mine I spent the last handful of years trying to make up for. At least, trying to stop things from getting worse.

The guilt hadn't let up, not for a moment.

"How did you know where to find him?" I asked. I wasn't going to deny his accusations, but I wasn't going to confirm them yet either. Honestly, I didn't think I needed to. We both knew what was going on here.

"I have my ways," Boner said. "I feel like I've told you plenty, and you haven't even given me your name."

"You've told me about myself," I pointed out. "Why should I believe you don't already know who I am?" Now I thought about it, he had zeroed in on me in the bar. It was possible he knew exactly who I was and targeted me because of it. Except, as far as I could tell, he hadn't run off to the cops.

Yet.

"This may come as a surprise, but I don't know everything," he said. "If you asked me who I thought I'd see sitting on a fire escape outside a window, you wouldn't have been on my list. But here you are. And here I am. Perhaps we can start over again."

He offered me his hand. "It's nice to meet you, I'm Boner."

Like I had with Cass, I tapped my fist against his.

"Harlow. Did you come here to kill this guy? I don't see any weapons on you."

"Would you believe I'm the weapon?" He grinned, white teeth flashing like the cocky prick he was.

"No."

"Ouch, right to the heart." He clutched at his chest. "You're right, I came with backup." He patted the pocket of his black leather jacket. "So, how do you propose we decide who does the honors?"

"I was here first," I said bluntly. "It would be better if you left so I could get on with it." I wasn't a big fan of leaving witnesses behind and it would be a shame to have to kill him. He did have a rather impressive boner.

"Funny, I was going to say the same to you," he said, completely unashamed. "Have you done this kind of thing before?"

I cocked my head at him, letting my red ponytail fall to the side. "Have you?"

"Are you asking me to incriminate myself?" He pretended to be offended.

"Seems to me you did that first," I said.

He reached up to scratch the side of his cheek. "You know, you're right. I apologize. Yes, I have done this kind of thing before. More times than I care to admit. And yet, not enough. Monsters like him still exist." His voice was lower now, regretful. Like he wanted to purge the world of evil with one swipe.

Yeah, didn't we all?

"Yes, they do," I whispered. I realized the man inside the apartment stopped pacing and talking. He must have ended his call. "His name is Carl. He owns a chain of hotels. In each one, he has a private suite where he has…" I had to take a moment to compose myself. "Girls delivered to him."

"I'm guessing this apartment serves that purpose too," Boner said, sounding disgusted.

"I was thinking the same thing," I agreed. "This place is too downmarket for someone like him."

"It still nicer than my place." Boner grimaced. "I propose we take care of Carl together. What do you say, Miss Harlow?"

"Miss St. James," I corrected. "Let's do this. I'm getting stiff sitting out here."

He grinned. "Funny, me too."

"Don't make me stab you," I told him. "Because I will."

He raised his hands in surrender. "I have no doubt you would. I'll try not to give you any reason." He nodded toward the window. "Ladies first? Or age before beauty?" He gestured to himself, then to me.

"I'm going first." I peeked through the curtain to

make sure Carl wasn't in the room just beyond the glass. I couldn't make out any sign of him.

Go time.

I jammed my knife into the side of the window, jimmying it open wide enough for me to ease it open and slip inside. All the while, I hoped like hell Boner was going to follow me and not stab me in the back. Literally. Just because I fucked the guy didn't mean I could trust him.

When I glanced back over my shoulder, he stood right behind me, inside the apartment. Relaxed, like he might be in a department store, shopping for his next pair of shoes.

"I'm guessing there's a bedroom over there," he whispered, nodding in that direction.

I made a face, but moved silently across the hard-wood floor, towards what seemed to be the only other room in the place. Stopped right before the doorway and glanced inside.

The room was empty. So was the bathroom off to the side.

"Mother of fuck," Boner said with an irritated grunt. "Where did the prick go?"

I put my knife away and leaned against the door frame. "He must have slipped out before we came in."

I flicked a switch to turn on the light and survey

the whole, small apartment. It was little more than a box. One that didn't look lived in, confirming my theory that this was somewhere Carl only spent small amounts of time. Him or his associates.

My stomach turned. What I was doing to Gary, what I had planned for Carl, it didn't compare to the evil these men did. For one thing, he deserved it. Their victims did not.

"I'll have to track him down some other way." I turned the light off again.

"We," Boner said absently. "I'm sure you'll agree, we're in this together now." He pulled open a drawer beside the bed, but closed it again when he found it empty. What was he hoping for? A black book full of incriminating evidence? Maybe a sim card?

"I disagree," I said. "I don't work with other people." Not in this capacity, anyway.

"This guy is—" Boner started.

He stopped when the door rattled.

Shit.

We both ducked down on the other side of the bed as the door opened. The light came on once again and Carl walked past us, carrying a pizza. He must have gone out to pick it up.

Of course, he wouldn't have food delivered here. Someone would see him. If he was recognized in a place like this, people would wonder at his presence.

Someone would film him and the Internet would do the rest. He'd be busted faster than a CEO at a Coldplay concert.

Although, what this guy was doing was far worse than cheating.

"Won't be long now." He seemed to be talking to the pizza as he set it down on the small table, just in view.

It didn't take a genius to figure out what he was waiting for. I swallowed before I lost the contents of my stomach.

Plates clinked together as he took them out of the kitchen cabinet and placed them beside the pizza. Only an arm and part of his leg in view, he froze.

"What the hell?" He noticed the open window.

Fuck, everything was going sideways. This operation was starting to feel like amateur hour, which wasn't like me at all. I *knew* there was a reason I didn't work with anyone else. Other people made messes, and I didn't like messes.

"Hey." Boner spoke loudly as he rose to his feet and stepped out of the bedroom. "Carl, right?"

What the hell was he doing? He was going to get both of us killed.

Or worse.

CHAPTER 4
BONER

"Great, you brought the food." I stepped over to open the pizza box and pulled out a slice. "Really, anchovies? What are you, evil or something?" Grinning, I took a big bite.

Okay, this was good pizza, anchovies aside.

"Who the hell are you and what are you doing here?" Carl stared at me. He inched toward the kitchen as though he was going to grab out a knife and use it on me. That wasn't going to happen. Not successfully anyway. Let him try. It'd be good for a laugh.

"Think of me as your unfriendly neighborhood vigilante," I said. "You see, Carl, I don't like people who do bad things to innocent people. They make humanity look bad. Do you want the aliens to keep flying past?" I took another bite of pizza and chewed.

"You're out of your mind." Carl backed away a few more steps.

"Actually, I'm very much *in* my mind," I told him. "Okay, I admit, I'm a bit flamboyant once in a while, but believe me, I'm all there."

Mostly.

I got a certain amount of pleasure from ending the lives of people like him, so maybe there was an element of unhinged going on here. Whatever, I was what I was.

"Whoever sent you, I'll pay you double," Carl said, his eyes wide. Pretending not to be scared but failing miserably, if you ask me.

"Here's the thing, Carl," I said slowly. I finished off the slice of pizza and wiped my hands on my jeans. "I don't get paid to do this. It's a free service I offer to the world. Generous of me, isn't it?"

"What do you want?" He backed up to the edge of the counter top. "Name your price and it's yours. A million dollars? Two million?"

I clicked my tongue. "Carl, Carl, Carl. I don't want your money." I paused for a moment. "No, that's not quite true. I'd happily take a couple million dollars. But not from you. Not while you're alive."

I snagged the pizza box from the table and held it out to him. "Hungry? This is pretty good. I mean, of course it is, this is New York City. Bad pizza would be sacrilege, wouldn't it now?"

I shook the box at him, but he looked back at me and didn't take a slice.

That's gratitude for you.

"What do you want then?" His eyes narrowed. "You want a share? You want some of my goods for yourself?"

I stuck out my tongue in disgust. "Did you just refer to girls as goods? And you wonder why I'm here. People like you don't deserve to live."

"You don't get to decide that," he snapped.

"Actually, yes, I do." I tossed the pizza back onto the table. "I get to decide exactly that. Isn't that grand? I get to be judge, jury *and* executioner."

Hell yeah.

His expression changed; he became borderline smug. "Did you really think I'd be here alone?"

"I don't see anyone else here," I said easily.

So far, Harlow kept herself hidden, probably wondering what the hell I was doing. To be honest, I was wondering the same thing. I could have waited until his back was turned, pulled out a knife and jammed it right into his neck. But this? This was more fun.

"They will be, any moment now," he said. "They'll walk right through that door behind you."

I jerked a thumb over my shoulder. "That door? No one is coming through the door." I stepped toward him. "No one is coming to save you, Carl. We'll see to that."

Carl looked understandably confused. "We? There's only one of you." But his eyes twitched, looking for something he might have missed.

"Yeah, you're right there, Carl," I said. "There's only one of me." Before he could look too relieved, I added, "But there's also one of her."

Right on cue, Harlow rose and stepped out of the bedroom.

She was dressed from head to toe in black, her red ponytail and pale skin contrasting with striking perfection. She looked like the goddess of death. Empress of fucking people up. Patron saint of making a man regret his life choices before taking their last breath.

And now my cock was hard.

"What are you doing?" she asked me. "I don't suppose it crossed your mind he might have drugged that pizza?" She raised one carefully shaped eyebrow at me.

"Of course it did," I protested.

That was why I offered some to Carl. Yeah, it didn't escape my notice he didn't take any. Still, if it was drugged, I'd be feeling it by now.

Wouldn't I?

"You wouldn't offer me poison pizza, would you Carl?" I asked.

Judging by the expression on his face, he'd do exactly that. In fact, right now he was wishing he had.

Rude.

Harlow moved over to make sure the door was locked and the chain in place. "We should get on with this. He's wasted enough of our time."

"Have some pizza," I offered. "You seem hangry."

"I'm not hangry," she protested.

She was hot when feisty. She was also hot mid-orgasm. A fact I hadn't managed to put out of my mind for the last couple of days.

"I don't like wasting my time." She gave me a look as though to accuse me of doing just that. As if it wasn't Carl's insistence on continuing to breathe that was taking up both of our time.

"You heard the woman," I said to Carl. "It's past time we dealt with you." I lunged at him, slamming one hand over his mouth and the other around his throat.

I wasn't the biggest fan of strangulation, it was slow and messy. In this case though, I'd make an exception. Especially given I believed him when he said he planned on not being alone for long.

Someone would be bringing the... 'goods' as he referred to them. Potentially multiple someones.

If there was something I didn't like to deal with, it was multiple someones, particularly angry, vengeful someones.

Carl struggled, but I managed to drag him down to the floor and pin him there. His eyes were wider now, starting to protrude from his head. So attractive.

Not.

"This is taking too long." Harlow dropped to her knees beside me.

"Tell him that." I squeezed his throat harder, but he was still kicking, arms flailing. "He's a stubborn prick."

She rolled her eyes at me, pulled out a knife and drove it straight into Carl's neck.

Narrowly missing my hand, mind you. In fact, I think she nicked off a piece of skin. It was hard to tell, with all the blood spurting out of Carl's throat.

"Has anyone told you patience is a virtue?" I asked her.

"I heard something about that once." She pulled out the knife and wiped it on his shirt. "I'm not in the mood to be patient."

"I noticed that," I said approvingly. She wasn't patient in jumping my bones either. A fact that was very good for my already healthy ego.

"I think you can let him go now," she said.

She was right. Carl stopped fighting and was lying still, making a mess on the floor with all that blood. I lifted my hand from his throat and patted his cheek.

"Nice talk, Carl. Although, to be perfectly frank, I prefer you like this." Cooling rapidly and unable to do anyone any harm.

"We need to get him out of here," Harlow said.

"Do you have a plan?" I asked, not trying to be facetious.

She was, after all, here first. A woman who planned to kill a man as big as this one must have figured something out in advance. Unless she was planning to leave him here to be found by the first unfortunate soul who stepped through the door. Which, if they were bringing an innocent victim, could probably not be considered unfortunate.

In fact, fuck them.

"I figured I'd throw him off the fire escape and go from there," she said.

"That would be a no then," I said.

She looked up at me sharply. "I would have figured something out. I always do."

"I'm sure you do." I glanced around before reaching for a towel which hung on the front of the oven. I wrapped it around Carl's neck before tucking the ends into his shirt. It was rough, but it'd have to do.

I didn't want to touch him, but I leaned over, picked him up and threw him over my shoulder. "Let's get out of here before his associate arrives."

"But if there's a—" she started.

"We deal with him, then we come back," I said quickly. "Do you know anywhere close by?"

"My restaurant," she said quickly.

"Your… Oh." Better not to ask too many questions at this point. Instead, I held on carefully to Carl and carried him out the door.

She stopped outside, so suddenly I almost ran into the back of her.

"What is it?" I glanced past her, down the hall toward the elevator. The place looked empty to me.

Wincing, she reached into Carl's pocket and pulled out his phone before pushing it into her own pocket at the back of her jeans.

"It might be useful," she said.

"Good thinking," I said. Keeping an eye out for anyone who looked like an evil associate, I stepped toward the elevator and pressed the button beside the aging mechanism.

"What was your plan?" she asked as we stepped inside and let the car take us down. "With him, I mean." She spoke carefully, clearly mindful of the possibility the elevator contained a camera.

"Same as this," I said easily. "It was inevitable. You know what Carl is like, he gets drunk and needs to be carried home. Sometimes, I'm tempted to throw him in the nearest dumpster and let him sleep it off." Like I usually did.

So far no one pinned any random bodies on me. Sometimes I wondered if they just weren't looking very hard. I mean, if anyone had an inkling of the things men like this got up to, would they want to bother? I knew I wouldn't.

Unfortunately, the cops didn't get to pick and choose, so no doubt they did look.

"Yeah, Carl is disgraceful," she said honestly. "He should be ashamed of himself."

"I'm absolutely certain he's regretting all of his life choices right now," I said.

Hopefully somewhere very hot and painful. With everything I'd done, I'd probably see him again someday.

The elevator pinged. We stepped out, Harlow leading the way, her gaze shifting back and forth, looking for anything suspicious.

Well, maybe not *anything* suspicious, because someone very suspicious walked right behind her. Me.

Rather, she was looking for someone completely devoid of a moral compass. I could claim to have one of those. Some people might disagree, but those people were mostly dead.

"It's possible he was bluffing," I said. "About there being someone else."

People would say anything if it meant avoiding a horrible death. Or even a slightly less horrible maiming. Carl might have planned an evening by himself in front of the TV, eating all that pizza. It was a lot of pizza for one person when I thought about it. Unless he planned to have some for breakfast.

In retrospect, I should have brought it with us. It was a shame to waste perfectly good food. Oh well, that couldn't be helped now.

Harlow hummed a sound of agreement and jerked her head toward the street, indicating that I should continue to follow. That was exactly what I did, whistling a lively tune as if I wasn't carrying a dead body over my shoulder.

Just another Thursday night in the neighborhood. Nothing to see here folks, move along.

Except Harlow's ass, which swayed as she walked. What were the chances of another round with the beautiful Miss St. James? Me and my cock were down for it if she was.

What can I say? Killing assholes made me horny. Also, spending time with pretty women like her made me horny. I had a lot more orgasms left to give, and I wanted to give them all to her.

And have a couple myself.

CHAPTER 5
HARLOW

"That always smells amazing." Erin leaned over from where she was slicing mushrooms and sniffed at the cooking meatballs. Eyes half closed, she inhaled deeply before leaning back.

"My father's recipe never disappoints," I said. "Especially with nice, fresh meat, delivered this morning."

Right before Boner went back to Carl's apartment. If anything else went down there, he hadn't come back to tell me. I couldn't decide if I was disappointed or not. He made last night more interesting, but messy as fuck. Although, the…disposal was easier with his muscles involved.

"Can I ask you something?" Erin tossed the mushrooms into a container and closed the lid. I'd use them later for risotto.

"Depends what it is," I said.

I gave the meatballs a final toss before turning off the heat to let them rest. Snagging a spoon, I stirred the sauce that would go over the meatballs and spaghetti.

She leaned her back against the counter. "I was thinking, I'd like to be more than a kitchen hand. Do you think I have what it takes to be a chef?"

I glanced over to her and slowly began to smile. "It's about time." When she gave me a confused look, I smiled more broadly. "I've been waiting for you to ask. If you didn't soon, I was going to give you a prod." I pointed the spoon in her direction and made a prodding motion with it, wincing as sauce fell off onto the tiled floor.

She laughed and hurried to clean it up while I went back to stirring. "So, you think I can do it?"

"I *know* you can," I said. "Are you thinking of leaving me?"

The expression of surprise on her face said she hadn't thought of that.

"I was hoping I could apprentice here," she said. "Between learning from you, and the culinary school two blocks over, I think I can learn everything I need."

She could do worse. I taught a few classes there myself from time to time. Their training was excellent. Of course, nothing compared to learning on the job, like I had with my father when he was still alive.

"If you want to train me, that is," she added quickly, her green-gold eyes now tentative. "I know I can be a handful."

I shook my head at her. "I'd be happy to train you. You're no more of a handful than anyone else I've trained." All two of them.

They'd both gone on to work at high-end resorts, probably making more money than I did. I was okay with that. I preferred to be my own boss anyway.

Besides, if I worked for someone else, it might be difficult to explain where some of the meat came from.

She let out a pleased squeak and gave me a sideways hug. "Thank you, thank you, thank you!"

"Yeah, yeah." I extricated myself from the hug and gestured to the other side of the kitchen. "You can start on making some more ice cream."

"Yes, chef." She saluted me before heading over and pulling the ingredients out of the fridge to make our semi-famous rum and raisin ice cream. Which was made with real rum and real raisins, nothing… unusual.

That reminded me of the meatballs. I stepped over to check the spaghetti, which hung on a rack to dry. I didn't really need to; I could make pasta in my sleep. I'd been doing it since I was five years old. First with my father in his restaurant, then with my mother at home.

"We have orders." Gina pinned them to the board and hurried away to pour water for the first of the lunch crowd.

I glanced at them before pulling spaghetti from the rack and tossing it into gently boiling water. A couple of minutes to cook and I tossed the pasta into bowls, added meatballs and topped them with sauce, before placing them for Gina to take to the customers.

I had to agree with Erin, they did smell good. Although, I could rarely bring myself to eat the meat I sourced myself. Dispensing of it was one thing, knowing what the 'animal' did was another.

Not that being an asshole was contagious, much less able to be transferred by mouth.

Still…

Gina grabbed the bowls and carried them over to the table. Smiling, she placed them in front of the customers.

"There you go!" She smiled and stepped away.

They retuned her smile and started to eat.

"Oh my God, this is delicious," one of them moaned.

"So good," the other agreed.

I turned away to start on the risotto and ravioli ordered by another couple of customers. The irony of watching the ravioli disappear under the water before it cooked wasn't lost on me.

Bye, Gary.

"I can't wait to make people moan like that," Erin said, looking out wistfully.

I glanced over and laughed softly. "How many times have you made that ice cream? They always moan over that." I jerked my head over to where the machine was happily turning away.

"But that's ice cream," she said. "Making everything else the way you do, that's what I want to learn."

I was certain she didn't want to learn to do *everything* the way I did. At nineteen, she was still relatively innocent. I wasn't going to shatter that for her. If she knew what I got up to at night, she'd probably be horrified.

I was, and I was the one doing it. I'd vomited the first time, but couldn't bring myself to stop. Not when I knew I was doing good in the world. As long as I stuck to people who deserved it, that would keep me this side of being a monster. Right?

"You can start by plating up the risotto," I said. The ravioli wasn't quite ready. That was what I told myself. It had nothing to do with not wanting her to be an accessory to the things I did.

Although, if she was going to do more cooking, it was inevitable. Unless I found a different method of disposal.

If Boner came around again, I'd ask him. He might have ideas I hadn't thought about. Methods he'd worked out that could work for me. Hopefully he would drop by. I really didn't want to involve Erin, if I could help it.

Of course, seeing him again had nothing to do with sex. It was all about covering my ass, not having him grab it.

That was what I told myself. I totally wouldn't picture him eating me out here in my own kitchen. No way. No matter how good the man was with his tongue. That was a one time thing.

End of story.

"Yes, chef." Erin hurried to spoon risotto into bowls and place them up as Gina appeared to take them out to customers.

"Your boyfriend's here again," Gina said, giving me a sly look as she grabbed the bowls and hurried away.

For a moment, I thought she was talking about

Boner, but then I looked out as Cass slipped into his usual chair.

Instead of a tablet, today he had a book in his hand. And bright pink earbuds, which he pulled out of his ears and pressed into his pocket.

He glanced over in my direction and grinned.

I ignored the strange thudding in my chest that could have been my heart and smiled back. Just a little bit. I didn't want him to think we could be anything more than casual friends. I shouldn't even let him be that.

I picked up a clean milkshake glass and held it up to show him I remembered what I said about giving him unlimited milkshakes. Even though I didn't think he'd actually sue me. A girl couldn't be too careful though, right?

I told myself this had nothing to do with me liking the guy, and everything to do with wanting to avoid scrutiny. Under the radar was right where I liked it.

He grinned bigger and nodded before picking up his book and opening it. He proceeded to stare at the page like he was reading the same line over again, distracted by… Probably the restaurant around him, not me.

Trying not to look too amused or interested, I

made him a chocolate milkshake with extra chocolate and carried it out to him myself.

It was the least I could do after throwing him onto the concrete. A bit of personal service went a long way. I learned that a long time ago. Some customers loved to be fawned over by the chef, the owner or both. If it kept them coming back, I'd indulge them when I had the time.

Especially if they were people I had my eye on anyway. Yes, we got those in here. They let me into their world just enough for me to take them out of mine.

"Compliments of the chef," I said as I set it down in front of him. "You know, we do a mean freshly squeezed orange juice and a virgin bloody Mary, right?"

We served wine as well, but he didn't look like a wine kind of guy. Or a drinking at lunchtime kind of guy.

"I'm sure they're great, but I like my hit of dairy and sugar," he said. He picked up the milkshake to take a sip through the paper straw. "I'm hungry today, what would you recommend from the menu?"

The look he gave me suggested he knew I'd see right through the question. He wasn't so much hungry as eager to keep talking to me.

"I can recommend the risotto," I said. "Or the

sweet potato gnocchi. That comes with a creamy, white wine sauce with fresh herbs." I wasn't going to tell them which herbs, I had to keep some things secret. But I did add, "And a hint of truffles."

At the same time, one of the customers from the table beside his leaned over and said, "My dude, you have to try the meatballs. I've never tasted anything like it. It's pork, or something like that, right?" He looked up at me questioningly, while holding his fork in his hand, one of the meatballs skewered at the end, almost dangling off the prongs.

"Something like that," I agreed. "With beef." Actual beef. I didn't say that last bit out loud. "Also with a hint of truffles." What can I say, I had a thing for them. They added a certain decadence to so many of my recipes. A quiet decadence. I made good food, not showy.

"I think I have to try to meatballs then," Cass said, totally oblivious to my wince.

Or perhaps he didn't see it, because I managed to keep it on the inside. I wouldn't be able to do half of the things I did if I didn't have a practiced poker face.

Ironic, because I sucked at playing poker. Personally, I preferred a good game of chess. Another thing my father taught me.

"If you're sure," I said. "The risotto is very good." It was my personal favorite, especially with loads of mushrooms and topped with Parmesan cheese. Even on my nights off, I made it for myself to eat.

"I'm sure," Cass said with a nod. "It comes highly recommended." He pointed his book in the direction of the other customer.

It seemed he'd made up his mind. I had to respect that. I liked people who were decisive. Usually.

"Right." I backed up a couple of steps before turning and heading back into the kitchen. Taking a deep breath, I put together a bowl of spaghetti and meatballs and gestured for Gina to take it over to Cass for me.

"You don't want to keep talking to him yourself?" she teased.

"It's getting busier," I said, which was the truth. Another two tables looked ready to order and a couple more people came in through the door.

"Okay, chef." She gave me a wink and carried the food over to Cass, her hips swinging while she walked.

I busied myself preparing meals as they came in, and carefully didn't watch him eat.

CHAPTER 6
HARLOW

"That was amazing." Cass stood beside his table, his book held against his chest, hair fallen over one eye as usual. He didn't seem to notice. If I didn't know better, I'd think he just got out of bed. He had that tousled look, wild and careless.

Gina and Erin both hurried around, packing up tables and taking dishes into the kitchen. Both pretending they weren't listening.

Both were listening.

"Yeah?" I placed his empty glass in the bowl, holding them carefully.

If there was something I disliked, it was dishes broken unnecessarily. It happened. Occupational hazard. I didn't want to be the one doing the breaking. Not when the replacement was coming out of my pocket.

"Yeah," he echoed. "It got so busy in here, but you didn't look like you broke a sweat."

Right, it was about me, not the meatballs. I should be relieved. It wasn't about the milkshake either. Shame, it was a particularly good milkshake, if I said so myself.

"I've had lots of practice," I said modestly. "You should see it here on a Saturday night."

"Is that an invitation?" he asked. "Do I need to make a reservation?"

He looked eager, like a puppy responding to a hint of cheese. Waiting and hoping to find some tossed his way. Ready to gobble it down in half a second flat and beg for more.

"No, and no," I said, frowning. "I mean, you can eat here if you want. We usually have a table or two spare if you're here early."

I spoke without thinking, blunt as ever. New Yorker, born and bred. It was who I was. I wasn't going to apologize for it, but sometimes I made myself cringe. For a moment.

Especially now, when he looked like I poked my toe into the side of his puppy. For the record, I'd never hurt an animal. I'd even been known to feed the ducks in Central Park once in a while. Proof I wasn't completely jaded, right?

"I'll make sure you get some garlic bread," I added, without knowing why.

I usually wasn't inclined to soothe a guy's ego, but Cass seemed genuinely nice. I wasn't used to genuinely nice. That had to be it. He had me on the wrong foot. Speaking without thinking. I'd have to watch myself around him. A guy like this could bring down carefully constructed walls if I let him.

In fact, he seemed like the kind of guy who would drag over a ladder, set it up against those walls and climb right on over. Maybe hide behind them with me. Maybe take them down from the inside.

I couldn't let any of that happen.

He perked up.

"I love garlic bread." He hesitated, glancing down at the floor. Without looking up, he cleared his throat and said, "When I was in college, I might have gone into restaurants for the free garlic bread and then bolted. I was kinda…broke."

He looked regretful now, like he might march into every last of them and offer to pay a couple of dollars for bread. I had a feeling he'd do it too. He'd get some funny looks if he tried. Bread was my loss-leader, the smell bringing in customers to buy more food.

If I relied on it alone to pay the rent, I'd go broke in a day.

"You and plenty of other college students," I said.

A couple of them came in here to do that too, but I always made sure they left with their stomachs full.

Erin was one of them, although she wasn't a student at the time. She was homeless after running away from her foster family. I'd taken her under my wing, found her somewhere to live and gave her a job. She repaid me by being like a little sister and sticking her nose into my business. The girl got away with far too much and we both knew it. We also both knew I'd continue to let her get away with it.

One day, when she was a Michelin star chef, she'd still get away with…well, not murder. Overstepping the line.

Pretending there was no line.

Erasing the line entirely.

Like I said before, I'm a bleeding heart. If I could save everyone like her, I'd do it.

Instead, I did what I could, one person at a time. While at the same time remembering to be grateful I'd never had to sleep on a park bench. Or know the pinch of an empty stomach. Not starving was one of the benefits of going to culinary school. We had to taste everything we made and there was always plenty to take home at the end of the day. For a couple of years, I lived on those leftovers, even the failures.

Especially the failures.

"What did you study?" I asked finally.

He pushed his glasses back up his nose and brushed his hair off his forehead. "You'll think I'm a total geek."

"I thought that when you sat there reading a book and eating lunch," I told him, teasing gently. "For the record, I'm not geek-phobic."

Especially when they were as adorable as he was. When I thought about it, he couldn't be more different from Boner, except that aura of darkness that lingered over both of them, and myself. Boner was blonde, athletic and a smartass, Cass didn't seem to be any of those things. So far.

Cass looked relieved at that. "I studied IT. I know, that comes as a complete shock, right?" He cocked his head and grimaced, his plush lips twisting to the side and pressing together.

"I would have guessed sports science, or business," I said flatly. He didn't look like the kind of guy who'd study either of those things and we both knew it.

"Thank you for not saying musical theatre," he said, making a face.

"You don't like musical theatre?" I asked.

"I love musical theatre," he said. "But that was what I did in my spare time, not as my major." His eyes widened. "Crap, did I say that out loud?"

"Yes, you did," I confirmed. "As it happens, I've seen *Wicked* five or six times, and *South Pacific* at least as many." I brushed hair off the side of my face and adjusted the bowl in my hand.

"The classics," he said wistfully. He half-closed his eyes and hummed a couple of bars of *I'm Gonna Wash That Man Right Outta My Hair*.

"You can sing," I said appreciatively.

His face reddened. "It helps when you're in productions like that."

I responded with a short laugh. "I suppose it would. I've been told my singing sounds like a cat being tortured, so I'll spare you from the pain."

Now I thought about it, that could be useful the next time I had a guest like Gary in my apartment. Singing, on top of dripping water, would have them pleading for mercy and offering up names much faster. I should have thought of that sooner.

On the other hand, I had some dignity left.

Sort of.

"I should—" I started to excuse myself, when Gina hurried past, taking the bowl out of my hand and taking it to the kitchen. Taking my excuse with her. The woman was such a brat.

"Have dinner with me?" Cass asked, the words tumbling out in a hurry, like a waterfall. Luckily, without the water or spray of any kind. "I mean, you get a night off, right?"

"The restaurant is closed on Monday and Tuesday," I said slowly. I usually used those days to rest and research my next guest or target.

"Of course she'll go out with you," Erin called from the other side of the seating area. "Go on, Harlow. You two are adorable together."

I looked over and lowered my eyebrows at her. I'd never make meatballs out of her, but she was toeing the line again. I shouldn't let her get involved in my personal life and I'd do the same in return.

Who was I kidding? Her and Gina got involved in my personal life all the time, and they weren't going to quit any time soon. How many times did they tell me to lighten up and have some fun once in a while? At least on a weekly basis.

What is it they say about how difficult it is to find good staff?

I looked back to Cass to see him look hopeful again. Part of me felt like I should go into the kitchen, slice some cheese and toss it to him in return for him sitting or rolling over.

"I can do lunch on Monday," I said finally. Lunch was more casual than dinner. A couple of people getting together in the same place to eat, not a date. No expectations. No pressure.

"It's a date," Cass said, throwing that idea right out of the open door and onto the street, where it was promptly run over by a taxi as the driver honked his horn at the car in front of him.

"It's not a date," I said.

"It's a date," Gina said hurrying past again.

"Definitely a date," Erin said gleefully.

"I don't suppose you know anyone who needs a job in a restaurant?" I directed the question to Cass, along with a sarcastic smile directed at Gina and Erin. They didn't need to see it, they'd hear it in my voice.

"I don't know, I think they're doing a great job," Cass said. Because of course he did. At the same time, he was obviously not trying to irritate me, he was genuinely happy they were on his side.

I know, they were trying to be on *our* side, but there was no *us*. There couldn't be an us. He was a nice guy and I was…

Someone who deleted men who did horrible things to girls and young women. Cass deserved better than someone like me.

"I can pick you up at your place," he offered,

pulling out his phone. I presumed to put my address in his contacts.

"I'll meet you," I said quickly. He definitely couldn't come to my apartment. Even with the Perspex box empty and put aside for now. It was better if he didn't even know where I lived. Safer for him and for me.

At some point the people I was targeting would figure it out and come after me. I didn't need him caught up in the crossfire.

"There's a food cart on the corner of Smith and Bradley," I said. "They sell the best pretzels in the city." Okay, that was one hell of a claim, but as far as I was concerned it was completely accurate. "I'll meet you there at twelve o'clock."

"I'll be there," he said, blinking a couple of times as though surprised I'd actually agreed to meet him anywhere. Maybe wondering if I'd actually turn up. Possibly trying to remember if such a food cart actually existed, or if I was trying to brush him off.

"I need to close up now," I told him. I grabbed the side of the door and gestured for him to step out so I could shut it behind him.

"Yeah, sorry." He stepped over hurriedly and almost tripped over the threshold on his way out. He windmilled his spare hand to stay on his feet. "This is getting to be a habit," he said when he righted himself. "You keep knocking me off my feet."

I ignored Gina and Erin's chorus of 'awww' as I smiled at him and closed the door before locking it.

I shook my head at myself and rubbed a hand over my forehead. What was I getting myself into?

CHAPTER 7
BONER

respect a woman who knows what she wants and goes after it. Even when it takes me by surprise. Which Harlow did when she told me to carry Carl into the back of her restaurant.

I asked no questions. Laid the guy down and went back to deal with his associate.

The associate who rudely didn't show up. Shame, I had energy to burn after spending time with her.

On the upside, I knew where to find her late Saturday night. Just as she was locking up her restaurant.

I waited until her staff left and leaned against the alley wall, where she wouldn't fail to see me.

"You need to stop showing up like this," she said, stopping in front of me, out of reach.

"Do I, love?" I asked easily. I crossed my ankles and cocked my head at her.

"Yes, you do," she said. "Wouldn't want to have any…accidents."

I grinned slowly. "Sweetheart, if you stabbed me, it would be on purpose."

She raised a single eyebrow. "Are you suggesting I should?"

That made me tip back my head and laugh. "Absolutely not. If anyone's doing any stabbing around here, it'll be me, with my cock."

"I told you that was one time." She started to walk past me.

My gaze lingered on her ass before I hurried to follow. "And I'm prepared to respect that."

She glanced over her shoulder. "Are you? First you appear on the fire escape—"

I held out my hands. "Total coincidence."

She continued as if I hadn't spoken. "Then you turn up outside my restaurant."

"Because you intrigue me," I said. "And I'm curious what happened to our…mutual friend."

Now she stopped walking and glanced around, making sure no one could hear. "What do you think happened?"

"Pizza topping? Baked Alaska? Wait." I pointed a finger gun at her. "Tiramisu?"

"Do you even know what those things are?" she asked, giving me a funny look.

Ouch.

I lowered my hand. "I know what pizza toppings are. Ground beef, ham, bacon. I'm a meat lovers pizza kind of guy."

"I'll bear that in mind the next time you eat at my restaurant on pizza night," she said dryly.

"On second thoughts, maybe vegetarian pizza," I hedged. Ridding the world of people like Carl was one thing, digesting him was another.

Harlow snorted. "Unless you have a better method of...disposal. This leaves less evidence behind."

"What do you do with the—" I stopped, aware I was speaking a little too loud. In a whisper I added, "Bones."

She winced. "This isn't the place to talk about it."

I grinned again. "I completely agree with you. How far to your place?"

"You're not coming to my place," she said, looking like she was over this whole conversation. "I have to go. I need to be up early."

"You can come to my place then," I offered. Because I'm nothing if not generous. "I'll make sure you get some sleep."

Eventually. Like I said, generous.

"Boner," she said with a sigh.

"Harlow." I mimicked her tone. "We had a good time the other night, didn't we? And by that, I mean both other nights. I like you, you like me."

"Who says I like you?" She cocked her head at me again.

"Why wouldn't you, I'm very likable." I smiled pleasantly. "Also, we have things in common. Things we can't talk about with other people. I bet there's plenty you want to get off your chest." For once, I wasn't thinking about her breasts, or even looking at them.

Mostly.

Let's be real, though. People whose hobbies included casual homicide also needed a shoulder to cry on. Why shouldn't she cry on mine?

Judging by the expression on her face, I hit my target right in the centre. There was no one she could talk to about the things she was doing. No one she could confide in who wouldn't run off to the cops in a heartbeat.

"You don't have to do this alone," I said softly. "We have the same goals. We want the same thing. Saving the world, one asshole at a time."

"Why?" she asked, her chin raised, eyes glittering in the light of streetlights and passing cars.

Why?" I frowned.

"Why do you do it?" She seemed to be caught right in the middle of backing away and giving in to her need to open up to someone. I couldn't tell which way she was leaning. I didn't think she knew either.

"Come to my place and I'll make you a coffee," I said, all sincerity now. "I'll tell you my story and you can decide if you want to tell me yours. If nothing else, you'll get a good cup of coffee. What do you say, love?"

She closed her eyes for a moment or two and exhaled slowly. "Fine. But only because I'm curious about you."

"Funny, I'm curious about you too," I said. And a lot of other things as well. This was about more than listening to her come, although that was a part of it. I'm only human after all.

"I'm sure you are," she said, her tone dry again. "Let's go then."

"Has anyone told you you're romantic?" I said, trying to keep a rein on my sarcasm.

"What could be more romantic than suggesting you try my pizza with special toppings on it?" she asked. "I wouldn't make that offer for anyone else."

"Does the aforementioned 'anyone else' know what they're eating?" I couldn't help asking.

She cast me a sidelong look that clearly said no, they didn't. "Shouldn't you be repulsed?"

"When you think about it, you're doing a service for the world," I said. "Save a pig, eat an asshole. And by asshole I mean…actually, both kinds." I slid a glance back her way.

"I figured you meant that," she said. "But you're right, I've probably saved a whole bunch of pigs."

"Do you eat…pork yourself?" Did I really want to know the answer to that?

"I'm not going to tell you all my secrets at once," she said.

"Right," I said slowly. "I'll tease them out one at a time as we go along."

We stepped out onto the street as a taxi cut off a car. When the light turned red, both drivers got out of their vehicles and started to yell at each other.

"Why don't you look where you're going?" one yelled.

"Fuck off, asshole!" the other yelled back. She dove back into her car as the light went green and drove off around the corner.

I loved this city.

"If only they knew, hmmm?" I smirked in their direction.

"They don't want to know," she said.

"That's the problem, isn't it?" I asked. "No one wants to know. Everyone is happy to look the other way when bad things happen."

"Not everyone," she said.

"No, not everyone," I agreed. "Not you and me. Not all heroes wear capes, right love?"

"I wouldn't call us heroes." She stepped over the contents of a spilled trashcan, grimacing at the contents.

"You're not squeamish, are you?" I teased.

"Of used diapers? Absolutely I am," she said. "They smell like they've been there for a week."

"Interesting," I said slowly. "Harlow St. James is squeamish."

"How do you feel about *being* a pizza topping?" She looked over at me.

"Negatively," I said. "As I imagine you do too. Unless you want your last act in this world to be saving another pig."

"When you put it that way, I feel selfish for declining," she said. "But I still decline. Not that I have any say in it." She stared off down the street, her expression dark.

"Is this one of those 'my days are numbered,' things?" I asked.

That was understandable. When you took the kind of risks we did, sooner or later something would go pear-shaped. Someone would fight back, or the cops would turn up at the wrong time. Or we'd lose what was left of our humanity and go on some kind of reckless spree. Something I was very mind-ful of.

It was another reason I wanted to be friends with her. For both of us to maintain our sanity. If we could avoid that occupational hazard, then I would. If I could help her, I'd be even happier.

"You don't feel that way?" She looked at me searchingly, like she was trying to figure me out. Fair enough, I'd been trying to figure her out since we met. I hadn't even scratched the surface of what made her tick. The more I saw of her, the more I wanted to see, know and understand. The more of myself I wanted to reveal to her in return.

"I don't think about it too much," I said honestly. "I get up in the morning, go to work, then..." I shrugged one shoulder. "Do my thing and go to bed. Then start the day over again."

"What do you do for work?" she asked. Of course she'd grab on to that. It was the most normal part of our conversation so far. Sometimes a bit of normal went a long way.

So I've heard. Don't quote me on it.

"I run an art gallery," I said. "Modern art, pottery, things like that. Sculptures made out of bones." I watched her carefully for her reaction. Someone who turned her targets into cuisine probably wasn't too worried about what happened to the bones.

She didn't flinch. "Animal bones?"

"What else?" In a public space like my gallery, human remains wouldn't go unnoticed. Shame, they'd make interesting sculptures. I could make a whole series, from Asshole Number One to Asshole Number… Whatever number I was up to.

Except, that wouldn't be terribly subtle. Did I do subtle? Not usually, but in this case I preferred to stay out of prison. I was too pretty for a place like that.

"Plaster," she said simply. "Or plastic like the skeletons you see in schools."

"I should be offended you'd suggest I'd have plastic in my gallery," I said with an exaggerated sniff. "The fact is, some of the work does contain it. But no, the bones are real. As real as I am."

"I'm not sure if that's the flex you meant it to be." For the first time tonight, she seemed to be holding back a smile.

"Touché, Miss St. James." I chuckled. "Were you an archer in a past life, or perhaps a sniper? You don't miss your target." I pressed a hand to my chest.

"I might be both of those in *this* life," she said cryptically.

"You just became twice as hot," I said. And my balls were now twice as heavy.

"And if I'm neither of them?" She cocked an eyebrow at me.

"I stand by what I said." I nodded. "You're twice as hot because you have a sense of humor. And if you can shoot, that's an added bonus. Especially with a bow and arrow. Think of it, we could start robbing from the rich and giving to the poor."

"That would be a twist on the Robin Hood tale," she said. "This is your building, isn't it?"

I hadn't realized we'd stopped until she said that. This woman was good at messing with my brain and I didn't mind it for a moment. Not with the memory of her pussy convulsing around my cock still fresh in my head.

Both of my heads, before you ask. One in a spin from being close to her, and the other I was struggling to keep from rising to full mast.

"Yes, yes it is." I pulled out my card and swiped it to unlock the front door and gestured her inside. None of this was as frantic as our night together, but it was early yet.

Smiling to myself, I followed her in.

CHAPTER 8
HARLOW

"So, what's your origin story?" I trailed my finger across the cracked linoleum. Clean, but the surface had seen better decades.

"What's the hurry, love?" Boner pulled two cups out of the cabinet and turned on the electric kettle. It started to gurgle loudly. I waited for his neighbor to bang on the wall, but if he was disturbed by the noise, he didn't let us know.

"Didn't you know curiosity killed the cat?" He spooned sugar into the cups.

"Lucky my name isn't Cat," I said, turning to look around the rest of the space. I hadn't been paying attention to it the last time I was here. It was cozy, with midcentury modern furniture, the couch and a narrow bookcase taking up most of the space.

"There's that sense of humor again." He pointed the spoon at me.

"Yeah, I'm a comedian." I walked over to the bookcase to peer at the titles. "Murder mysteries and Stephen King. Why am I not surprised? Is this your inspiration?"

He laughed. "Nah, that's what I read for fun. They keep me grounded."

I turned around and pressed my lips together as if I didn't quite buy it.

"Why do you do it?" I tried again. Most people didn't wake up in the morning and decide to sneak into someone else's place to kill them. The decision to do that was gradual. We weren't opportunists. We planned. Chose our targets. Justified what we were about to do, to ourselves.

Then we did it.

Boner closed his eyes and exhaled, his jovial mask dropping away.

"My father used to get rough with my mother. She always made excuses for him, but the only excuse was that he was a stone cold asshole." He opened his eyes and looked down at the floor. "She always had bruises. Then, one day he died."

"You killed him?" I guessed.

He looked up at me and laughed humorlessly. "No. Dickhead got into a fight at the pub. Copped a punch right to the face. Fell and hit his head on the footpath. Sidewalk, whatever. Died in a puddle of blood. But my mother? It was like she came to life when he fucked off. She mourned him."

He shook his head, clearly not understanding why. "She grieved, then she blossomed. Like she deserved to, you know? I decided then and there I wouldn't let anyone bully a woman if I could help it."

"How old were you?" I asked.

"Fifteen." He glanced over to the kettle which was almost ready to whistle. "When I was seventeen, I was walking home late one night. Saw a guy trying to rape a woman. Threw him off a bridge."

He shook his head just slightly. "There was remorse, yeah, but there was something else too. Relief. Asshole couldn't hurt anyone else. And the woman, she could go on with her life without being broken the way he would have broken her."

"The first one is always the most difficult," I said. I understood why he did what he did. Not only that, I would have done it too.

"See, I didn't find it difficult," he said. "I guess I was six ways of fucked up already. I hate to admit I might be just like my old man."

"Bullshit," I said. "There's a big difference between someone who hurts an innocent person to make themselves feel better, and someone who hurts guilty people to make the world better."

"Is there?" he asked. "I could have called the coppers. I could have punched the bloke instead of hurling him off a bridge. I could have fought him off her and taken her out of there."

"You also could have walked past and done nothing," I argued. "Plenty of people would have."

"Plenty of people suck," he grumbled.

I laughed bitterly. "Those are some facts you're speaking there. But there's also lots of good people in the world. People who need other people looking out for them."

"People like us," he said. When the kettle clicked off, he poured hot water into both cups and added milk before handing one to me.

"People like us," I agreed as if he'd offered that as a toast. "So you graduated from throwing assholes off bridges to hiding on fire escapes."

"Huh, I must have missed the part where I get a cap and gown. And my pretty degree from Vigilante University." He gestured toward an empty space on the wall with his cup.

"At least you don't have to pay back the tuition," I pointed out. "How long have you been here?"

"Here in the states, or here in this shit hole? Actually, the answer to that is two years. My mother remarried and I figured I could use a change of scenery."

"Is she happy now?" I asked.

He smiled as he said, "Yeah. Alan is a good bloke. He treats her like she's a queen. Which she is, if you ask me."

He clearly adored his mother. Which I had to admit was cute as hell.

"I'm happy for her," I said honestly. "Every woman deserves to be treated like a queen."

"Even badass vigilantes." He nodded toward me. "Especially beautiful ones with red hair and mean knife skills."

"I don't know about that," I said, sipping my coffee.

"I do." He finished off his drink and put the cup down beside the sink. "I don't think I've met anyone who deserves as many orgasms as you do."

"That's very specific," I said, trying not to think too much about our night together. It was good. Very good. A repeat performance wouldn't be a hardship. What it would be though, was a complication. Those scared me more than anything.

"It's very accurate," he said. He took my empty cup from my hand and placed it beside the other one. "You're a gorgeous woman, Harlow St. James." He ran his knuckles down my cheek, across my neck to my throat.

"So fucking pretty." He leaned in and kissed me lightly, barely more than a brush of lips over lips. "Go out with me."

"On a date?" I frowned at him, but my heart was thumping away in my chest.

"Yeah. Dinner, movie, a walk through the park. The works. You are allowed to eat at other restaurants, right?"

"They usually don't object to me walking through the door," I said, pretending to misunderstand what he was asking. "And I don't mind eating other people's cooking either. I'm always curious about the way other chefs use flavor. Once in a while, I learn something new."

"Huh, I never thought of that," he said. "I can understand though. Like an artist is always open to appreciating new art forms. New ways to work with light or new materials. Like animal bone versus plaster."

"Life is a learning experience," I said. Right now, I was learning about my body's response to being so close to him. Remembering the way his piercing felt inside me didn't hurt either.

He cocked his head and smiled. "See, that's what I keep saying. The moment we stop learning is the moment we might as well curl up in a sad ball in the corner, because we've essentially given up. And no one ever said Edward Douglas Bonegard was a quitter. I bet they never said you were one either."

He hesitated for a beat and a frown before asking, "How did you come to own your own restaurant at the tender age of..." He gestured at me to fill in the implied blank.

"Twenty-eight," I said. "Family money. Inheritance, to be specific. It's given me a lot of freedom to do the things I wanted to do."

"So it's true what they say, money is the root of all evil." But he was grinning as he said it.

"Money is the key to a lot of things, including freedom and, to some extent, evil," I agreed. "Rich people get away with a lot of things." Now I was thinking back to Gary and Carl. Both rich men. Both who used their wealth to do abhorrent things.

"Sometimes they don't get away with them," Boner pointed out.

"Eventually," I said, letting my frustration show. They'd gotten away with plenty before I caught up with them. Others were doing the same thing as we stood here talking.

"Better eventually than never," he said. "So, about our date. When are you free?" He looked certain I'd make the time.

I remembered I was having lunch with Cass on Monday. I didn't want to string either of them along, but I hadn't made any promises. Why shouldn't I go out and enjoy myself with two different, attractive men? It wasn't as though anything was going to come of it anyway.

We'd have a nice time and then go our separate ways. Maybe we'd be friends afterward, maybe we wouldn't. Maybe we'd fuck, maybe we wouldn't do that either.

"I'm free Tuesday night," I said finally. "Let me know where and I'll meet you. Unless you want me to pick a restaurant?"

I knew the restaurant scene of the city pretty well by now. Especially those within a three or four block radius of mine. Between us, we covered every kind of cuisine you could imagine. And some you couldn't. Some were about creative presentation as much as they were about feeding diners. That wasn't my thing, but I appreciated the artistry. How could I not, when their food looked so elegant?

"I know a place," he said. "It might not be up to your standards, but it's pretty good. And I'm almost certain they don't serve asshole."

"Only *almost* certain?" I asked, arching an eyebrow at him.

"I'd like to be one hundred percent, but you never

know." He grinned, clearly sure the restaurant didn't source meat the same way I did. He was probably right. I'd like to think I was an exception.

"I'm going to need your number so I can text you the address," he said.

I considered refusing, but he already knew where my restaurant was. If he couldn't text me, he'd turn up in person, possibly at the wrong time.

I held out my hand for his phone and put my number into it. Before I handed it back, I called myself so I'd have his too. Otherwise, when he called or texted, it would come up as a unknown number, and I didn't answer those. Did anyone, these days? It's almost as though the 'phone' part of telephones had become redundant. Now we used them for anything but making phone calls.

"Good girl," he said, taking the phone back and tucking it away in his pocket. He cupped my cheek and smiled down at me. "Now, you were going to tell me your origin story."

"Was I?" I asked. "I'm not sure you're ready for mine." I'd never confided any of it to anyone. I wasn't sure how I felt about doing it now. It might help, getting it off my chest, but it might also bring back a world of demons. Demons I thought I'd put behind me. Now I wasn't so sure.

After all, they were the reason why I did everything I did.

"Sweetheart, if you haven't noticed, I'm always ready for anything." One side of his mouth tugged up, along with both of his eyebrows.

"You don't think I could catch you off-guard?" I asked. "That sounds like a challenge to me."

"I always like a challenge," he said. "You can try. Why don't you start at the beginning. See if you can shock me."

"Do you mind if we sit down?" Without waiting for an answer, I lowered myself down to his couch. I waited until he was sitting beside me before I started to tell him the whole, sordid story.

CHAPTER 9
HARLOW

"My father started his working life as a chef." I leaned against the back of the couch. "By the time he was thirty, he owned two restaurants. Those two became a chain. Eventually, he retired from working in the kitchen and concentrated on the back end."

I ignored Boner's smirk.

"Turns out, he was an even better businessman than he was a chef. He expanded into hotels and then real estate. Went from being a regular guy to multi-millionaire."

"So your father is Batman?" Boner asked.

I snorted. "Hardly. My father was ambitious. For every dollar he made, he wanted two or three more. It became something of an obsession to him."

"Rumor has it, that's how rich people get rich," Boner said. "They do everything they can to get more money."

"Exactly," I said vaguely, thinking back. "The more money he got, the less time he had to spend with my mother, my sister and me."

"I have a feeling that's not a bad thing." Boner looked at me sidelong.

"Looking back, it wasn't," I agreed. "At the time, it stung. He taught me how to cook. With regular meat," I added quickly before he could ask.

"That you know of." He gave me a sly grin.

"Yeah, well." I shrugged. I couldn't discount the possibility entirely.

"Go on," Boner encouraged. "Daddy turned into an obsessed workaholic, what happened then?"

I grimaced at that description, accurate though it was. "He made some powerful friends," I said slowly. "The kind of people who think they own the world because they have money and influence. People who think they can do anything they want."

"People like Carl," Boner stated. "Bottom feeding assholes."

He looked like he'd happily bring Carl back to life and kill him all over again. I could relate to that. Death seemed too good for some of these people.

Which was why some ended up in my party box, with slow dripping water.

"Right," I said softly. I glanced away, seeing nothing, lost in my own thoughts.

"What did he do?" Boner asked gently. Carefully, he placed his hand on my knee, lightly at first as though I might jump at his touch.

Considering what was going around and around in my brain it was a fair bet. One I managed to win by not jumping.

"He thought he might make some money from my sister and me," I whispered. "Lettie was a couple of years younger than me. Absolutely beautiful. She could have been a model, but she wanted to work with animals instead. She planned to be a veterinarian. She was the sweetest person I ever knew. She had the biggest heart."

"Had?" Boner asked gently. "Past tense?"

I didn't acknowledge that he'd spoken, not yet. I continued talking, letting the words out one by one.

"My father thought he'd sell both of us. But she was the one they wanted." I could barely speak above a whisper. Saying all of this made it real again. Like it only happened yesterday.

"What did they do?" Boner whispered.

I turned to him. Let him brush tears off my cheeks.

"They raped and murdered her." My voice broke on the last two words. "The sweetest person on the face of the planet and they destroyed her. Broke her into pieces, just because they could." My heart broke all over again.

I closed my eyes, moisture pooling on my eyelashes.

"I made it my life's work to destroy them," I said, managing to contain my composure just enough to be coherent. "Starting with my father. So far, I've found three of the others."

"Jesus Christ." Boner's hand tightened on my knee before he forced himself to relax again. "How many?"

"Including the man who organized all of it, seven," I said. "He didn't touch her, but he was behind it. Her and so many others like her. Whoever he is, he lives in the shadows. I suspect he's very powerful, very rich. He thinks he can't be touched."

So far, he was right. The three men I found hadn't been able to give me his name. Or weren't willing to. Even knowing they were about to die, they were too scared to tell me.

"So, we're looking for three bottom feeding assholes," Boner concluded.

It took a few moments for his words to register.

"We? There is no we." I shook my head.

"Sweetheart, you can't tell me all about this and

then not expect me to be involved up to my eyeballs." He held his hand up in front of his eyes. "These are exactly the kind of scum sucking shitworms that need to be brought down. If there was a Vigilante University, its mission statement would be to get rid of them. Like it or not, I'm in with you on this. Besides, it might help to have another pair of eyes when it comes to finding the head asshole."

I ran the pad of my thumb across the nails on my opposite hand, back and forth while I tried to think up some argument that would convince him to forget all about this. I should have realized telling him would lead to him inserting himself into my... mission, for want of a better word. Crusade.

"I appreciate you wanting to help," I said slowly, "but this is my revenge. They need to pay for what they did to my sister. It's been too long already."

"Revenge is a dish best served cold," he quoted. "In this case, revenge is very much a dish." He actually winked at me.

"I've never been called a dish before," I said.

"Then the men in your life were doing you a disservice," he said. "Go on then, let me help you. Otherwise, I'll be forced to follow you around and join in wherever I can."

"Did you just threaten to stalk me?" I asked.

"Are you shocked I'd do something illegal?" He quirked an eyebrow at me.

I had to concede that point. Edward Bonegard wasn't what you'd call a law-abiding citizen. Me either, so I couldn't judge.

"You're going to get in the way if I don't let you help me, aren't you?" I asked. "Like you did with Carl."

Boner pretended to look offended. "I was very helpful. Perhaps you have a selective memory." He said it with no heat and a hint of a smile.

"I had everything under control," I said. "But if you really want to help, I guess I could use another pair of eyes and hands. We might find them and end them quicker. Before they can do it again." I wasn't naïve enough to think they haven't already done it again. And again. We could stop more of it.

"Can I ask you a question?" He ran his thumb back and forth just above my knee.

"Can I stop you?" I asked.

"Usually, not," he agreed. "Believe it or not, I have some boundaries and this may poke at it too much. If you don't want to answer…"

"Since I can't stop you, you might as well ask," I said dryly. I made an 'out with it,' gesture with my fingers.

"You said your father tried to offer both of you," Boner said carefully.

I guessed where this was going. "You want to know if he succeeded. No, I killed him before it got to that. As far as I know, no money exchanged hands."

"And your mother?" Boner asked, a wince already on his face.

"She passed away before all of this happened," I said. "I like to think she would have stopped it, but I'll never know." It was obvious he thought she'd had a part in it too. That was clear from the flash of relief on his face.

"I'm sorry you lost your Mom," he said after a moment. "Moms are special. Dads, they should be special too." A hint of a smile tugged at the corners of his mouth. "Was yours the special of the day?"

I snorted. "He had a regular old cremation," I said. "It was ruled an accident."

That made Boner grin. "Good girl. Nice work. He was your first?"

"Yeah, he was." I gave a short nod.

At the time, it was the most difficult thing I'd ever done. Looking back, it didn't seem like that big of a deal. It hadn't brought my sister back, but inheriting all his money gave me enough to start my restaurant. And buy a nice condo. I'd kept some aside for expenses, but donated the rest to women's shelters around the city. Who the hell needed that much money anyway? I certainly didn't. I left myself enough to be comfortably off, but not ridiculously rich.

"I'm starting to think we need a T-shirt," Boner said. "Card-carrying members of the Daddy Killers Club."

"That would be subtle," I said sarcastically. "T-shirts and membership cards."

"A support group then," he said, unflinching.

"Isn't that what this is already?" I gestured toward him. "A support group for serial killer vigilante daddy murderers."

"That sounds like a great title for a movie." He grinned. "Serial Killer Vigilante Daddy Murderers." After a beat he added, "From Mars."

I snorted a laugh. "Speak for yourself. I'm not from Mars. Before you say it, I'm not from Uranus either."

He tipped his head back and laughed. "There's no way someone as cute as you could come from Uranus, or mine. Although, if we're going to talk about anal…" He wiggled his eyebrows, then moved to kneel in front of me, between my thighs.

"Boner," I whispered.

"Harlow," he whispered back. "You deserve orgasms. Let me do this for you." He placed his hands on my thighs and ran them up slowly, until his thumbs were almost pressed against my pussy.

"I don't want you feeling sorry for me because of what my father did," I said. "Or for what I did to him."

"Good, because I don't. You're a badass. You don't deserve pity, you deserve respect. You deserve pleasure." He rubbed his thumbs up and down slowly over the fabric of my leggings, teasing me.

When I didn't object, he hooked his fingers into the waistband of my leggings and panties and pulled them both down. He leaned in and inhaled.

"You smell sweeter than honey," he whispered. He nudged my clit with his nose, then replaced it with his tongue, teasing and lapping slowly. "You taste even better."

I pressed my hands to the couch on either side of me, closed my eyes and let him feast on me.

As much as my instincts wanted to tell me to keep my distance from him and everyone else, he had a talented mouth. One that was going to make me come undone faster than I could have done myself with one of my well-designed toys.

"You're dangerous," I said softly.

He looked up at me and grinned. "You're just figuring that out now, love?"

"No, I noticed it on the night we met, but you're good at reminding me," I said.

"I'm good at a lot of things." He slid a finger inside me. Just one at first, spreading my arousal around my pussy. Then, in went another finger, and a third. Massaging my G spot while his tongue worked my clit.

I arched my back and looked toward the ceiling, my eyes glazed, all of my senses focused on the man between my legs and the attention he was lavishing on my pussy. I barely had time to suck in a deep breath before I was coming hard and fast against his mouth. Panting and crying out his name.

Ignoring the neighbor banging on the wall again.

If anything, I cried out louder because of his irritation. That was what he got for trying to ruin a perfectly good orgasm. Honestly, he was probably listening, his hand wrapped around his own cock. Hoping I'd shout louder still.

I flopped back down against the couch, trying to catch my breath.

"Just like that," Boner said approvingly. "You're incredibly beautiful when you come." He eased my panties and leggings back into place and patted my knee before moving to sit beside me again.

He leaned over to lightly kiss my mouth, letting me taste myself on his lips. "So fucking perfect. Now, we need a name for this plan. How about Operation Revenge?"

He switched gears so fast, he almost gave me whiplash. I blinked a couple of times and shook my head to clear it, so I could catch up with him.

"We can think about that," I said.

He nodded slowly. "Okay, that's fair. Now, where do we start hunting for these assholes?"

CHAPTER 10
HARLOW

saw Cass long before he saw me. He sat on a bench, one knee jiggling as he looked around anxiously. Every so often, he pushed his glasses back up his nose. For once, his hair wasn't over his face. Only when I was close enough, I could see he had it held back with a small, black clip.

He was so adorable, I almost turned around and walked away.

Right before I could, he turned and saw me, his whole face radiating with a smile.

He leaped to his feet and hurried toward me, eagerness in every step.

"I wasn't sure you were coming," he said, giving me a hug that seemed to envelop my entire body. Maybe part of my heart and soul as well. It was warm, generous, and I surprised myself by not wanting it to end.

I found myself putting my arms around him and hugging him back before stepping away.

"I'm sorry, I should have asked first." He winced with his whole face, everything from his mouth to his eyebrows getting in on the action.

"It's okay," I said. "If I didn't like it, I would have said so."

"Right. Yeah. Okay. Of course." His eyes widened and his face turned pink. "Sorry, I'm so awkward sometimes. All right, all the time. Especially around women who are as pretty as you are." He ran a hand over the back of his neck. "I won't be offended if you want to leave."

No, he wouldn't be offended, but he'd probably be hurt. There I was, once again thinking about his ego.

I wasn't going to stay to soothe his ego. I was going to stay because he was refreshingly sweet. A stark contrast to the rest of my life. That was a good reason why I should walk away right now, but I couldn't bring myself to. I shouldn't be using him for a few minutes of normality. That was what I was doing, right? It felt like it.

"I'm good," I said. "Let's get pretzels?"

He smiled. "Yeah." He took my hand and we

walked toward the pretzel cart. It wasn't until we got there and he pulled out his wallet that he realized he was holding my hand.

I thought he was going to apologize for that, but he didn't. He must have known what the answer was. If I didn't like it, I would have taken my hand back.

Honestly though, I liked it. It was another piece of normal in my otherwise crazy existence. Almost as if we were regular, everyday people.

If only he knew how irregular I was. He'd probably take off running for the hills. For now, we could enjoy each other's company, right?

"What kind of pretzel would you like?" Cass asked. He looked at me like he half expected me to choose a gourmet option. Fair enough, considering what I did for a living. When it came to pretzels, I had simpler taste.

"Plain with salt," I said.

He nodded and turned to the man who worked the cart. "Three, please. Actually, make that four. I'm hungry."

He was giving me the impression he was the kind of guy who was always hungry, ate a lot and never put on so much as a hint of fat. Like a growing, teenage boy.

Once again, I was reminded of an energetic,

golden retriever. One who ate everything in sight before running circles around everyone. Literally.

"I can pay for mine," I started to say, but he already tapped his card and paid for everything.

"Fuck," he whispered, his card halfway back to his wallet. "I feel like I'm really screwing this up."

"You're not." I put a hand on his arm, surprised by how hard his bicep was. Apparently he did other exercise as well as running around in circles. A lot of it, from the feel of him.

"I owe you for all those milkshakes and lunch." He pushed his wallet into the back of his dark jeans and handed me the bag of pretzels.

"Let's call it even." I opened the bag, pulled one out and handed it back to him. The delicious scent of baked and boiled bread tickled my nose, making my mouth water.

"Deal." He pulled out a pretzel for himself and tapped it against mine, like we were toasting something. He took a bite and half-closed his eyes, groaning at the taste. "You were right, these are the best pretzels ever."

"Of course I'm right." I bit into mine and chewed, appreciating mine a little more subtly. "I know my pretzels."

He chuckled and led me away toward a food

truck, this one serving—to the surprise of no one—milkshakes.

I shook my head when he asked if I wanted one, but he ordered a chocolate shake, the bag of pretzels tucked under his arm while he had his hands full with food and drink.

"It's not as good as yours." He sipped. "But it's still good."

"You really like those, don't you?" I ordered a soda and paid for mine before he could.

"I've never met a milkshake I didn't like," he agreed. "You must think it's weird. A guy my age still drinking milkshakes."

"I can't say I have an opinion about other people's drink choice," I said. "If that's what you like, the only person whose opinion matters is yours. Besides, you're not the only one your age who drinks them. Why do you think I have them on the menu?"

"For kids who eat there?" But he seemed to like my answer.

"For *anyone* who eats there," I said.

We found ourselves back at the bench, where we sat and ate in silence for a couple of minutes. Watching people walk past.

Tourists with phones in their hands, taking photos of, and with, everything. A couple of dads walking past hand in hand, a kid to either side of them. A couple of older women, laughing about something as they wandered past. Several bicycles carrying food orders. The usual hustle and bustle of the city.

"You've lived here all your life?" Cass asked. "I mean, you said you know your pretzels. I got the impression…"

"You got the right impression," I said. "I was born here. Never lived anywhere else."

I looked over at him. "I've travelled around the country and a bunch of other countries. I've never found anywhere else I wanted to live." I was almost certain my sister's killers still lived here. Or did business here. Even if I wanted to leave, I couldn't. Not until her memory was finally put to rest.

"What about you?" I asked.

"I've been here for about a year," he said. "I came from the West Coast. I needed a change. So I applied for a job here and I got it."

"There's not many changes bigger than moving to the other side of the country," I said.

"Sometimes it feels like a different planet," he said. "But I like it here." Color creeping up his cheeks again, he added, "I like it even better since I met you."

"You must really enjoy being flipped onto concrete," I said wryly.

"I didn't hate it," he admitted, mumbling a little. "It's not every day you get flipped by a beautiful woman."

"Are you sure about that?" I asked, teasing gently. "A guy like you, you probably have women lining up to flip you."

That drew a chuckle from him. "If there is, I don't know about it. I bet you have men lining up to be flipped."

"If there is, I feel sorry for them," I said. "If being flipped is the best they can get…"

Cass laughed. "You'd be surprised. Some of us can only hope to get flipped."

He put down his pretzel on his lap and placed his hand on his forehead. "You must think I'm the lamest lame that ever lamed. The cringiest cringe to ever cringe. The… You get the idea."

"I don't think you're lame or cringey," I assured him. "I think you're sweet. Sometimes it can be difficult to meet people."

I didn't get the impression he was the kind of man who lived in his parent's basement, spent all day playing video games and then wondered why he couldn't get the attention of a woman. He was awkward, but he had no problem putting himself out there. Like he said, he wasn't good at social cues. That didn't stop him from trying.

"When I first got to the city, I was working sixteen-hour days," he said. "The only people I met were people from my office. They're nice enough, but even if I was interested, office romances can turn ugly." He pulled the straw out of his milkshake and drank the rest straight out of the cup.

"That's totally understandable. I don't want to date anyone I work with either," I said.

Of course, they were all women, but that was beside the point. He was right, things could turn ugly. It was easier not to go there. Especially when I was the boss. If they didn't quit, I'd have to fire them, and I always struggled doing that. Yeah, killing people was easier than letting them go. I know exactly how fucked up that sounds.

"Could you see yourself dating me?" Cass asked. "I mean, this is kind of a date, but maybe, I don't know, something more intimate."

I should have turned him down flat right now for both our sakes. Told him we could be friends and that was it. Stood up right now, walked away and hope he didn't follow. Whatever it was between me and Boner was complicated enough already, right?

Even so, I found myself saying, "I like you."

"I like you too." His smile was soft and full of hope. "So, dinner? I could cook for you. It won't be as good as your cooking, but I'd like to think it's edible."

No. Absolutely not. It was a terrible idea.

"I'd like that," I said, the words coming out of my mouth, which seemed intent on ignoring my brain. "I'm sure whatever you cook will be delicious." I admit the idea of someone else cooking for me was appealing. As much as I loved to cook, doing it every night got tedious.

His eyes widened. I could almost see him thinking, scrambling. Trying to figure out why he offered to cook for a professional chef. But then realizing even if he fucked it up completely, we could order food to be delivered. It wasn't the meal that mattered, it was getting to know each other.

Which, in spite of myself, I wanted.

"Tell me where and when and I'll be there," I said.

"Next Monday?" Once again, he looked relieved and hopeful at the same time.

"It's a date," I said.

What are you doing? I asked myself. The only answer I could give myself was that I was getting to know a normal guy, hoping like hell I didn't ruin his life.

Considering who I was and what I did in my spare time, I was going to have to be incredibly careful.

In spite of myself, I was looking forward to it. Maybe I could juggle normal and avenging angel.

Somehow.

CHAPTER 11

HARLOW

was being followed. I knew by the way the back of my neck tingled. Goosebumps broke out on my arms.

At the next set of lights, I crossed to the other side of the street, using the reflection from car windows to look behind me. For a moment, I thought it might be Cass.

Then I saw him.

He wasn't really trying to be subtle. Of course not, that wasn't his style. It still begged the question, why the hell was he following me? That was definitely what was going on here. Someone like him didn't just happen to be walking the same way I was.

I stopped suddenly outside a shoe store and admired the display in the window. A girl could never have too many boots. And theirs were particularly nice. Did the red ones come in my size? They'd go perfectly with my black skirts.

I glanced over my shoulder to see him walk past, the momentum of the crowd carrying him forward. To his credit, he didn't look back at me.

Reluctantly, I stepped away from the window and followed him. All the way to the end of the block before he turned onto a side street.

Keeping my distance, I took the same turn, almost running straight into him.

"Why are you following me?" His dark brown hair was cut short except a small section on the top. That was almost long enough to curl. Eyes almost the same color as his hair demanded answers, but without fear or anger. Instead, there was a need to know. To understand.

"You were following me," I pointed out. "I should be asking you that question."

"I wanted to know where you were going," he said, as if somehow that explained everything.

"Why does Archer Hardwick want to know where I was going?" I cocked my head at him. "Why do you give a shit?"

"Curiosity," he said simply. "Why else does anyone do anything?"

"I can think of a lot of reasons," I said. "I'm not sure curiosity even makes the top ten."

"I saw a post on social media the other day that listed curiosity as the third reason for why people did most things," he said.

I shouldn't have asked, but I couldn't seem to help myself. "What were the top two reasons?"

"The second reason was greed, the first reason was cats." He shrugged one shoulder.

I snorted a laugh. "That sounds like a good reason not to believe everything you see on the Internet."

"Cats aren't a reason for why you do the things you do?" Again, he seemed genuinely interested in the answer.

"I can't say they are," I said. "I haven't had a cat in a long time."

"Maybe it's lack of cats," he said, as if this was somehow a rational conversation. "You want to get a coffee?"

"I could use some caffeine," I said. "There's a café on the corner back there." I jerked my thumb over my shoulder.

He peered around before pulling out his phone and swiping at the screen. "The reviews look good." Decision made, he pushed his phone back into his pocket.

Shaking my head at him, I made my way through the press of people until we slipped into chairs opposite each other, beside the window. Where I could watch people passing and coming in and out. With a wall directly behind me, I could see everyone and everywhere.

Yes, it was paranoia, but I preferred to be ready.

"What brings you to this part of the city?" I propped my elbows on the table and looked over at him.

"The usual," he said easily. "I heard on one of the police channels about a man who broke his daughter's arm during visitation. Figured I'd show him how it felt." He didn't add 'before I kill him.' It was implied, and we both knew it.

We met after I killed my sister's second killer. Archer had come to do the same thing. We'd cleaned the place up in silence and had breakfast together afterwards. We struck up a friendship of sorts. As much as people like us could have friends.

"Have you finished with him?" I asked carefully.

"A little over an hour ago," he said. "In approximately eleven hours, the police will be informed. They'll find him in front of the TV, watching reruns of *CSI*."

"How ironic," I said.

Archer cracked a small smile. "I thought so. I saw a meme the other day that said how much a person would hate to die while listening to a singer they didn't like. Because the people who found them would assume they liked them. This guy was more into hard-core porn than he was into *CSI*."

"That's funnier than it should be," I said.

"I was going to put his TV on a kids channel, but that seemed wrong." He spooned four sugars into his coffee and gave it a stir. "Not to mention suspicious."

"Right, a guy found in front of his TV wouldn't look suspicious at all," I said sarcastically. From what I knew of Archer and his techniques, the man's death wouldn't be ruled a suicide. More likely, he had his throat cut.

"At least he won't be sullying *Sesame Street*," Archer said, sucking coffee off his spoon.

"Or hurting his daughter," I said.

"That too," he agreed. "So, who's the pretzel guy?"

He waited until I took a sip to ask that. I had to swallow while trying to think of how to respond.

"He's a friend," I said.

"He wants to be more than a friend," Archer observed.

"He might," I said evasively. "Are you trying to keep tabs on me?"

"Just an observation," he said. "I was going to come over and say hello, but you know the saying: two in every three people wish the third one would go away. I figured it was better to wait until he was gone. I didn't want to interrupt your date."

"It wasn't a date. Not exactly," I said, scratching behind my ear. I had a flower tattooed there. A lily. For no other reason than I liked them.

"He looked like he thought it was a date." Archer sipped his coffee. "You want me to talk to him? Get him to back off?" He was a little burlier than Cass, with a similar, dark air. An undercurrent of barely controlled violence. Archer knew his way around a knife and wouldn't be remorseful in drawing blood.

"No, I don't want you to talk to him," I said quickly. "I like him. He's sweet."

"Does he pick up his own socks?" Archer asked.

I gave him a funny look. "I have no idea. I've never been to his place. Why do you care about his socks?"

"I read a study once, where if women started to pick up a man's socks at the beginning of a relationship, they'd be doing it until the end of it. Therefore, a guy who already knows how to pick up his own socks will be less of a challenge." Archer made it all sound so reasonable.

"Do you pick up your own socks?" I cocked my head at him.

"Is that your way of asking me out?" He drew his brows together. "So you can find out if I can pick up after myself?"

"That's some mental gymnastics," I teased. "I

already know you can pick up after yourself. I've seen how meticulous your cleaning is."

"Are you asking me to marry you?" His expression was perfectly deadpan, only his fingers moving as they gripped his coffee cup. The rest of his arm, fully covered in a sleeve of tattoos, was perfectly still. "Because I sound like the perfect mate from your description."

"Did you read that online too?" I asked.

"Probably. The Internet is an endless source of information and entertainment." He brought his cup to his lips, looking back at me before taking a sip. "Three and a half stars. Not bad, but not great."

"The Internet is an endless source of something," I said, taking a sip of my own coffee. "For the record, no. I'm not asking you to marry me. I have no intention of marrying anyone." I waited for him to quote some random statistic, but he didn't.

"I have to confess, I was following you," he said. "Not just because of pretzel man."

"His name is Cassius," I said. "Cassius Titmus. Why were you following me?"

Instead of answering, Archer pulled out his phone and tapped Cassius' name into the screen.

"I didn't tell you that so you could stalk him," I said.

"Is this him?" He turned the phone around so I could look. "He has a golden ratio face."

"He has a what now? Yes, that's him." Cass was wearing a suit and sitting in front of a computer, looking like he wished he was anywhere but having his photo taken.

"Golden ratio," Archer said as if that would explain everything. "It's a mathematical proportion that determines attractiveness. You have a golden ratio face too."

"Um, thanks? You're not so bad looking yourself." It seemed like the thing to say.

"My face isn't symmetrical enough." He placed his phone down.

"I feel like I should say you shouldn't put yourself down," I said. Now I was looking more carefully, his nose did tilt a little to the left. So did his chin. One of his ears was bigger than the other. Not noticeably so, but still.

"Just being realistic," he said. "If I was bothered, I'd have surgery to correct it. As it is, I really don't give a shit."

"Good, I think that's a healthy way to look at it," I said. "We are who we are. And if we don't like it, we can get tattoos and piercings." I raised my arm, almost as covered in ink as his. Each of my ears was pierced four times in different places and my septum was pierced, although I rarely wore any jewelry in it.

"Exactly. What about matching ink?" He squinted at me. "You said you'd never get married, but would you get matching ink with someone?"

"I don't know," I admitted. "I've never given it any thought. I mean, ink is permanent and sometimes relationships aren't. I'm not sure I want that reminder on my skin forever."

"What if the relationship doesn't end?" He propped an elbow on the table and rested his cheek on his hand. "If, statistically, fifty percent don't last, then fifty percent also do. Those odds aren't so bad."

"Yeah, well." I shrugged. "I can't see myself getting involved in anything long-term with anyone. If I do, I'll figure it out then."

"You still have your tally?" He gestured toward my forearm, just below my elbow.

I pushed my sleeve back to show a row of seven lines, three with a strike mark through them. There was nothing to suggest what they meant. If you knew, you knew. If you didn't, you could guess because chances were I wouldn't explain it. He only knew because I told him as we were cleaning up after our mutual kill. Back then, I only had two lines struck through.

Archer nodded. "I have some information that

might cross another one off. That was why was following you. I wanted a chance to talk to you."

"Some people call or send an email," I pointed out. Considering how attached he was to his phone and using technology, wanting to talk in person was somewhat contradictory.

"Someone might intercept it," he said. "The Internet is always listening. Have you ever searched for something, only to see ads for it turn up on your social media feed? This was better done in person."

He was right. He couldn't exactly send me an email saying, Hey babe, I found someone you're trying to kill, let's go and murder them.'

"Okay, so what—"

I was interrupted as Boner slipped into the chair beside us.

"Hello love, this is cozy."

CHAPTER 12

BONER

was walking past the café when I saw Harlow sitting with a person I didn't recognize. Call me a nosy bastard if you like, but I had to slip inside and make my presence known.

Maybe it was some irrational irritation at seeing her with someone else. I'd like to say I don't do jealousy, but frankly that would be bullshit. When it came to this woman, I did jealousy in spades. Also in hearts, diamonds and clubs. As far as I was concerned, she was the whole pack. All fifty-two cards, even if that made me a joker. I prefer to think of myself as a king, personally.

But I digress with the playing card metaphors.

I smiled at her, then at him. Naturally, the one I gave him was less than toasty warm.

"You two aren't plotting the demise of humankind, are you?" I asked.

Let's face it, if anyone was going to do that, they might as well do it in a café.

"Not the whole of humankind," Harlow said. "Just select members of it."

"Not me, I hope." I waved down a server and ordered a cappuccino. "Are you going to introduce me to your friend?" I nodded to the tattooed man in her presence.

They exchanged a glance, both nodding like they were giving each other permission to share information in front of me. As if I wasn't perfectly reliable.

I could be offended, but I had better things to do than waste time on an emotion like that. I really was the epitome of irrational.

"This is Archer Hardwick," Harlow said. "Archer, this is Edward Bonegard."

I stuck my hand out toward him. "Everyone calls me Boner."

"Everyone calls me Archer." He shook my hand briefly before taking his back.

"I'm sure they do." I grinned.

I'd bet the kids at school gave him grief for his last name. They did the same with me, but I chose to embrace it. After all, what was wrong with a perfectly good erection? So what if they couldn't get their cocks up? That wasn't my problem.

"What were you two so deep in conversation about?" I placed my arms on the table and leaned forward, looking from one to the other and back again. "Whose demise are we plotting?"

The server gave me a funny look before placing my coffee in front of me, but hurried away. No doubt she heard worse in a place like this.

Harlow said, "Someone like Carl," at the same time as Archer said, "You should stay out of it."

Once again, I looked from one to the other. Harlow was so gorgeous, I had a hard time looking away from her. But if they were talking about someone like Carl, then I wanted in.

"Sorry pal," I said to Archer. "I'm already involved. Whatever the beautiful Miss St. James wants me to do, I'll do." I turned back to her. "What do you need?"

"I don't know yet," she said. "Archer was going to tell me what he knew."

She looked at him expectantly.

He looked at me like he wished I'd go away.

I looked at him like he better tell her whatever he was going to tell her or he'd have me to answer to.

She rolled her eyes at both of us, which was fair.

"Not here," Archer finally said. "Somewhere more private."

I jerked a thumb at him while my eyes were on Harlow. "You trust this guy?"

"I trust him as much as I trust you," she said.

"That much, huh?" Okay, that might have meant she didn't trust either of us, but I choose to take it differently. If only for the sake of my ego. Yes, yes, it's not fragile, but I have my moments, all right?

"My gallery is just around the corner," I said. "We can talk in there and not get interrupted." I was on my way there anyway. I'd ducked out for an hour or so to meet up with a new artist, but I needed to get back. Not that the place would fall down without me, but I liked to be there to oversee sales as much as possible. I liked when money changed hands, especially when it was coming straight to me. Okay, me and the artist. Still, money.

Archer looked doubtful.

I leaned toward him and said, "I'm not going to use your bones for a sculpture."

He leaned toward me and said, "I might use yours."

Our faces were maybe an inch apart. Close enough I could smell the coffee on his breath.

I grinned. "Perfect. I've always wanted to be a work of art."

"Are you saying you aren't already one?" Harlow teased.

I turned my face toward her and grinned bigger. "Now you mention it…"

"I read a study once that said unattractive people think they're more attractive than they are," Archer said flatly.

Rather than be offended, I raised an eyebrow at him. "What did it say about people who actually are attractive?"

"You don't have a golden ratio face," he added.

"Mine's more of a fraction than a ratio," I said. "It's a fraction more attractive than yours." I punctuated that statement with a smug smile.

"Studies have shown that English food is ten times more bland than any other cuisine," he retorted.

I barked a ha. "Now you're just making shit up. Next thing you'll say the Earth is flat. Or the moon landing was faked."

Sure, English food was uninspiring at times, but it wasn't that bad. After all, who didn't like a pie floating in pea soup, with a side of chips and a glass of Guinness?

"There's no air on the moon for a flag to wave." Archer shrugged. "But the Earth can't be flat or cats would knock everything off."

I laughed out loud at that. "You know what, you're an odd bloke, but you're funny."

"I have an eidetic memory. Sometimes it comes in useful." Archer picked up his phone from the table and started to look at something on the screen. "Is this your gallery? Bonegard's? Average rating of a bit over four stars. Not too bad." He seemed unimpressed, like the kind of guy who was hard to please, unless it involved hot wax and one of those drawers like they have in the morgue.

Don't ask.

I ate the chocolate off the top of my cappuccino with a spoon and stirred the rest before taking a sip. "Can't say I pay too much attention to online reviews. Art is subjective, so all of that is only opinion anyway. One customer loves the things another customer hates. If I decided everything I did based on shit like that, I'd never do anything. How fun would that be?" No bloody fun, if you asked me.

"This review says the floor was sticky." Archer's face was expressionless.

"A kid dropped a lollipop," I said. "We've had it cleaned up since."

I'd never known the stickiness from a lollipop to spread as much as it had that day. I could have come all over the floor and made less of a mess. And had more fun.

Figures someone would take the time to leave a review about that. Granted, it was fucking unpleasant. We kept a closer eye on young visitors after that. And any who looked like they might take the chance to come all over the floor. If anyone was going to do that, it was going to be me. Preferably with help from Harlow.

"I'd like to see your gallery," Harlow said.

"Of course you would; you have good taste," I told her.

Now I was going to have to think how to get rid of Archer as quickly as possible so I could show her all the spots that were good for fucking. I had quite a few ideas. She probably had a few of her own.

Once she realized I really wasn't going anywhere, she might open up more and we could try different things. I was patient. She'd be worth it.

"The sooner we go, the sooner we can be done," Archer said as if that wasn't abundantly clear. Maybe we were on the same wavelength after all.

My coffee was a little too hot, but I drank it all down, savoring the way it scalded my esophagus and brought tears to my eyes. I appreciated a bit of pain. It made me feel alive and reminded me of the people I killed. They were dead, I wasn't. I needed to appreciate that more than I did.

"I'll pay," I said. If Archer was going to give

Harlow the kind of information I was hoping for, he was doing us a favor. The least I could do was to pay for his coffee.

Before he could argue, I was up and off to the register, leaving a generous tip for the server. Like I always did, because I drank here several times a week at least. They looked after me and I returned the favor. Besides, the coffee here was almost drinkable. That deserved recognition.

I turned around to tell Harlow and Archer to follow me, but they were right behind me. So close I almost bumped into them.

"Getting up close and personal, I see." I grinned.

"Sorry." Harlow put her hands up and stepped back.

"Don't be," I told her. "I like being up close and personal with you." I wanted to kiss her right now, but if I did, I might not be able to stop. I suspected the staff wouldn't appreciate if I sat her on one of the tables and ate her out.

Or would they? We might have to find that out another time. When Archer wasn't lurking nearby, casting the occasional glance at Harlow. He probably thought I didn't notice, but I did. It was obvious to me he had a thing for her. That was fine with me, as long as it didn't get in the way of me and her.

I grabbed her hand and pulled her to the door and out onto the street. The buzz of the city immediately ignited a matching buzz through my whole body. You couldn't help noticing it wherever you went. The air was thick with it. Constant motion and energy.

The only time I wasn't borderline manic was that moment after one of my victims took their last breath. Then, a heavy stillness overtook me, from my toes to the top of my head and deep into my soul. A sense of peace I couldn't get any other way.

It was almost as good as an orgasm.

I led them through the crowds, right up to and inside my gallery.

It was quieter in here, soft music playing through the speakers, lulling people to linger and part with their cash. The air was set to a perfect temperature, a hint of lavender fragrance drifting through. The only thing missing was a small fountain with a tinkle of water. I might have to look into piping that sound through the speakers too. Anything to lull visitors and give them that sense of well-being that kept them here for longer.

I led them into my office and gestured for them to sit on the comfortable leather chairs while I perched on the desk.

Harlow sat back and crossed her legs at her knees,

her hands resting in her lap. She looked comfortable, like she belonged here.

Archer, on the other hand, was also perching, glancing around himself like a sword might come flying out of the wall and decapitate him.

That was ridiculous. I didn't need a sword coming out of the wall. I kept a garrote in my top drawer. And a knife. And, if push came to shove, a gun in the second drawer.

No one ever said Edward Bonegard was unprepared. If they did, they didn't say it for long, because I proved them wrong. The dumpster out the back was emptied regularly, I saw to that.

"Okay, what's this about 'someone like Carl?'"

CHAPTER 13

HARLOW

Archer gave Boner the side-eye. A sentence I wouldn't have imagined thinking a couple of weeks ago.

"We can trust him," I assured Archer.

"Yeah, you can," Boner said. "Out with it, Hardman."

"Hardwick," Archer corrected.

Boner flapped his hands at him. "Whatever. Spill the coffee."

"Don't you mean spill the tea?" I squinted at him.

"I don't like wasting perfectly good tea." He grinned at me, then gave me a wink.

Archer sat still through all of this, his expression unchanged. Somewhere between unimpressed and slightly bored. His hand twitched like he wanted to scroll on his phone while we were bantering.

Another minute or two and he'd probably whip it out.

His phone, that was.

"So anyway," I said. "Archer, you have a lead on someone we need to deal with."

Staying impassive was a challenge. If he knew something, knew *someone* that was doing terrible things to women and girls, I wanted to deal with them then and there. Before they could do anything else. I'd had to learn patience over the years, but I still didn't like it.

"We know the names of the first three men who took your sister," Archer said slowly.

I nodded. I hated saying them out loud, but I'd said them in my head over and over so many times it was like a classic rock track in the back of my brain. An earworm.

"Fred Alonzo. George Wentworth. Oscar Hetherington." I wanted to vigorously brush my teeth to get the taste of those names out of my mouth. Maybe step into a hot shower and scrub my skin until it was raw.

Boner turned his face slowly to stare at me. "You're the one who ended George Wentworth? I knew you were hot. That guy gave scumbag slugs a bad name. Tell me he died slowly." His eyes were wide, eager for the gory details.

"Very slowly," I said. "He had some regrets in the end." As for me, I had none. Except to wonder if he suffered enough.

Boner rubbed his hands together. "I fucking love that for him. I wish I was there to see it."

"If you're lucky, you might be there to see the next one go," I said, nodding for Archer to continue.

"One of my contacts found a connection between them and a man named Granger Fairfield," Archer said. "It seemed like they operated in a pack. Sometimes with several girls between them, sometimes with one."

I knew all of that, but it still made me sick to my stomach.

"Any chance you've been able to find the other three?" Absently I rubbed the tattoo on my arm.

"No." Archer's usually guarded face now showed a hint of regret. "I've tried asking around, but if I poke too much, they'll know we're looking."

"We?" Boner asked. "Are you two…" He flicked a finger back and forth between me and Archer.

"Friends," I said at the same time as Archer said, "Associates."

We exchanged glances.

"Associates," I said at the same time as Archer said, "Friends."

Boner grinned. "Either way, we're doing this

together, yeah? Taking out Granger Fairfield." His body was tense, poised like he was ready to head out the door and tear Fairfield apart right now.

"What we're not doing is running in half-cocked," I said.

"I only ever do things full-cocked," Boner said, dropping his gaze toward my pussy. "I'm sure you remember."

Archer gave me a look, his brow creased. "Three of us going in there might be overkill."

"It sounds like the perfect amount of kill to me," Boner said. "What else do you know about this asshole? For example, can you confirm he was involved in what happened to Harlow's sister? Or any other girl, for that matter? I don't go around killing indiscriminately."

Archer gave him a flat stare like he didn't believe that for a moment.

"Even if you do, I don't," I said. "Boner is right. We need to be absolutely sure we have the right person."

"Right," Archer agreed. "At this point, I only have what my contact told me. I searched Fairfield up." Of course he did. "He stands to inherit his father's jewelry empire. On the surface, he's squeaky clean."

"In my experience," Boner said slowly, "the squeakier someone is on the outside, the dirtier they are on the inside. They always seem to be overcompensating, trying to cover up for their fucked up-ness."

"Studies have shown that the image someone presents has a profound impact on the way others react to them," Archer said. "These men were, and are, up-and-coming businessmen. They want to portray an air of success. They want to seem untouchable."

"All the better to get away with anything," I said bitterly.

"They aren't getting away with this," Boner said. "Three of them already haven't. The rest must be sweating in their knickers." He almost seemed to relish the idea.

To be honest, so did I. Had they wondered if the first three deaths were related? Did they know there was a possibility someone was coming for them?

If so, we had to be even more careful. I hated to admit it to myself, but it might take three of us to succeed. I didn't usually work in pairs or packs, but if it meant bringing down Granger Fairfield, then so be it.

"So, first thing, we need more information on this prick," I said slowly.

A thought slowly formed in my mind. I wanted to dismiss it, but it made too much sense.

"Men like these often keep incriminating things

on their computers," I said reluctantly. "If we could hack into Fairfield's, we might find..."

I couldn't finish that sentence. We all knew what we might find. Images none of us wanted to look at. Things no one should see. If we found what I suspected we would, those girls deserved justice. Closure. I couldn't give them back their innocence, but I could give them this.

"Let me guess, you know a guy?" Boner asked.

"I might," I agreed. "I don't really want to bring him into this, but..." I uncrossed my legs and crossed them the other way.

"If he can get us into Fairfield's computer, he doesn't need to do anything," Archer said. "Better if he doesn't. Then, if the cops come after us, he won't know anything."

"Hardcastle is right," Boner said. "All we need is access. For all we know, Fairfield doesn't have anything like that stored away."

"Hardwick," Archer corrected. "He might have some other incriminating evidence. Something that'll tie him to Lettie St. James."

"And if we don't find it, we follow him," I said.

"If it comes to that," Archer agreed. "Getting past his security is going to be the biggest challenge."

"I love a challenge." Boner looked ready to tackle

it head-on. "I always say to myself, Edward, either you win again or you die. There is no losing."

"Dying sounds like losing to me," Archer said. "I read once that people are aware for about seven minutes after they die. Seems like you'll have time to think about whether you're winning or not."

"Sounds like bullshit to me," Boner said easily. "Hey, I have an idea."

"I'm not going to die so we can test the theory," Archer said. "If you're offering…"

"No one is going to die here today," I said, raising my hands, palms facing them. "Let's focus on Fairfield. He's the enemy, not anyone in this room. Okay?"

"You're right," Boner said. "Sorry, bro." He leaned forward and offered Archer his hand.

"Yeah," Archer said with a sigh, but he leaned forward and shook Boner's hand. "Can I have a few minutes alone with Harlow?"

Boner's gaze slid to me, his expression skeptical.

"It's okay, I trust him," I said.

Archer could have called the cops on me a long time ago. I could have done the same to him. Of course, neither of us could do that without incriminating ourselves. No, if he wanted to, they would have shown up on my doorstep a long time ago.

Mischief in his eyes, Boner slid his gaze back over to Archer.

I sat forward and poked Boner in the side with my fingernail. "He trusts me too." He really would do almost anything for a laugh.

"Yes, I do," Archer said. The look he gave Boner clearly said if there was anyone in the room he didn't trust, it was the Englishman. Fair enough. They'd known each other for barely an hour. That was a short amount of time for anyone, much less people like us.

Trusting the wrong person could get us thrown in solitary confinement the rest of our lives.

Or worse. No, I don't mean death. I mean being buried alive, up to my neck and left there to die slowly. Or locked in a sensory deprivation tank. I know those are specific, but I have particular nightmares.

"Right then." Boner placed his hands on his thighs and hopped off the top of the desk. "I'll leave you crazy kids to it for a few minutes. Don't make my floor sticky." He looked meaningfully at Archer, but he was smiling at the same time, right before he strode out the door, closing it behind him.

Archer rubbed his temples with his thumb and forefinger. "Where did you find that guy?"

"Ironically, about the same place I found you," I

said. "We both had the same target." I decided not to mention the night we spent together before that. Archer probably figured out by now that Boner and I had fucked at some point. I didn't need to give him the details.

"You really trust him then?" He glanced at the door as if he suspected Boner was on the other side, listening. Considering how thick the door was, I doubt he'd be able to hear a word. No, if he was listening, it wasn't through the door.

"Yeah, I do," I said. "He's a lot, but he's one of us. If he wasn't, the cops would be breaking down the door."

I'd taken note of the amount of cameras in the gallery. Just because I couldn't see evidence of a listening device in the office didn't mean there wasn't one. If he'd called them the moment he stepped out of the office, they'd be here by now.

"I guess so." Archer didn't look convinced.

"You two will learn to get along," I assured him. "I don't want to have to pick a side. You know what will happen then."

"You'll pick homicide?" A smile tugged at the corners of his mouth.

I grinned. "Exactly."

He chuckled softly. "Can I take you out some time? Make up for our coffee being interrupted." He seemed surprised at himself for asking, but made no attempt to take the words back. If anything, he seemed relieved they were out there, in the world.

"Sounds like I need to take *you* out," I said. It *was* my friend who interrupted us after all. I owed him a raincheck. "After we hack Fairfield's computer?"

"It's a date," he said. "But let me pick the place. I know a guy. I'm almost ready to go after him. We could do it together." His dark eyes shone with a fierce light, like he came alive when he was planning a kill. Like everything else was monotonous right up until the moment he sliced skin open.

"That's so romantic," I said, teasing lightly. I wouldn't say no. If we were going to go after a big, difficult target together, then some practice wouldn't hurt.

Well, it wouldn't hurt *us*.

"I should go and talk to Cass," I said. I surprised myself by how much I was looking forward to seeing him. It wasn't all about asking him to hack Fairfield's computer for me. I genuinely liked the guy.

Which, frankly, was terrifying.

CHAPTER 14

HARLOW

walked the couple of blocks to Cass' building. The doorman let me pass and make my way up to Cass' apartment. I was about to knock on the door, when it swung inward.

He stood with his hand on the knob, smiling at me. "Hey. Sorry, I saw you through the peephole." He jerked his head toward it.

"Were you standing there watching?" I teased as I stepped inside.

"I choose not to answer on the grounds I might incriminate myself," he said. He closed and locked the door behind me. "Dinner is almost ready."

"It smells delicious," I said sincerely. The apartment was filled with the smell of garlic and spices.

"One of the few things I know how to cook are

tacos," he said apologetically. "I was hoping you didn't mind something so basic."

"I love tacos," I said. "If my restaurant wasn't Italian, it would have been Mexican."

"My two favorite cuisines," Cass said. He stepped over to the stove to stir the sauce that was bubbling away there. "And Chinese."

"Mine too," I said. "With a bit of Spanish and a lot of French thrown in for good measure."

"Talking about food like this is making me hungry." He opened a box of taco shells, and the plastic wrap around them as well. He jerked his head to flick his hair out of his eyes. "Would you like something to drink? I have beer, or soda. Or milkshakes."

A milkshake maker had pride of place on his counter.

"Beer sounds perfect," I said. "Thank you."

He opened the fridge, took out two beers and a bowl of what looked to be home-made guacamole. He set the bowl on the counter and handed me a beer.

"My mother's recipe. She refused to let me leave home without being able to make it." After a beat he added, "I refused to leave home until I knew how. I could sit down and eat an entire bowl of it."

I twisted the lid off my beer and tossed it into the trashcan beside the counter.

"Guacamole is a basic life skill, if you ask me. It's like knowing how to boil an egg."

"Or make coffee." He took a sip of beer before placing the bottle down and turning the heat off from under the chicken. Leaving it to cool for a few moments, he pulled out sliced tomato, more avocado, shredded lettuce and cheese.

"You've been busy," I said as he laid out everything so we could fill our own tacos.

"I'm sure you slice prettier than I do." He pulled a couple of plates out from the cabinet and handed one to me.

"At work, my knife skills have to be meticulous." Both at the restaurant and when dispatching predators. "At home, I'm a little bit rougher. Between you and me, it tastes about the same."

Not exactly the same. There was a reason for the uniformity in a professional kitchen. At home, I was never so fancy that I was going to police his vegetable and fruit-cutting skills.

I loaded up my taco with everything and sat down at the small table beside the kitchen.

"This is really good," I said after swallowing my first bite. "If you ever decide to stop working in IT, you can come work for me."

Pink crept up his cheeks. "I'm sure it's not that good."

"It's excellent," I assured him. "One of the best tacos I've ever had. And I don't go around saying that about any old taco."

"You should try my enchiladas some time," he said. His eyes widened when he realized that could be construed as an innuendo.

I laughed softly. "I'm sure your enchiladas are delicious."

I was drawn to him, I couldn't deny that, and not just for his enchilada, or because he might be able to help me to give my sister justice. There was something about this guy that made me want to be around him. Like a moth to flame, perhaps. Although, in this case, I was the flame and he was the one who might get burnt to a crisp.

His face was redder now. "Would it be wrong if I said I wanted to taste your burrito?"

I couldn't stop myself from smiling, both at the euphemism and the expression on his face. Like he couldn't quite believe he said that.

"Thank you for not calling it a fish taco," I said dryly. "But, no, it's not wrong to say that. I'm a big fan of asking for things you want. If you don't, then how do other people know what's on your mind?"

I cocked my head at him before taking another bite of taco.

"You're not like anyone else I've ever met," he blurted out. He pushed his glasses back up his nose with the back of his hand.

"I could say the same about you," I said. "In fact, I *would* say the same. It's refreshing to meet someone who isn't all about himself, you know?"

"I know what you mean," he said. "Most of the women I've met are all about themselves. Men too. They care more about the likes and follows, even when they're not online. They're out to impress everyone. I just… Want to be myself."

"Me too," I agreed. "Tell me more about yourself. I know you work in IT. Have you ever hacked into anything?" I kept my tone light, like I was joking, but my heart was racing.

Surely he'd see right through me and hate that I was trying to use him? I hated myself for it. I would have liked nothing more than to explain exactly why I asked.

I couldn't. Doing that would drag him into something he didn't deserve. Something that might destroy him. I wasn't going to be the one to do that.

He laughed. "It's part of my job to know all the tricks of hacking into other people's systems. That's how we prevent people from hacking us. In theory, anyway."

"You don't put those skills to use outside work?" I asked. "I don't think I'd be able to help myself. Imagine how many secret sauces I could discover."

He looked confused. "You don't need to find out someone's secret sauce."

"No, you're right," I conceded. "But I could keep people from hacking my restaurant computer and discovering all my secrets."

"You have a problem with people doing that?" Now he looked annoyed on my behalf.

I decided to take the opportunity he offered. "All the time. The competition is always trying to get a step ahead of me. A few times, I've had to change my recipe because they've found out what I was using. As soon as they spread it around, no pun intended, I have to switch my game up." That was all true. The restaurant industry was cutthroat sometimes.

"That sucks." He got up to make himself another taco before sitting back down. "Is there anyone in particular who's doing this to you?"

Feeling like garbage for continuing to lie to him I said, "There is. Granger Fairfield."

Cass frowned. "The jewelry mogul?"

I cursed myself. I should have realized there was

a chance he'd heard of Fairfield. Hell, for all I knew, he worked for him.

"He has his fingers in a lot of pies," I hedged. That was true for lots of men like Fairfield. No doubt it was one hundred percent correct. People like him loved to dabble in restaurants and hotels. Anything that might make them more money.

"Okay," Cass said slowly. "Will you let me take a look at your computer? I can see if anyone's gotten in there and put some things in place so they can't do it again."

"Will it involve hacking into his systems?" I asked, trying not to hold my breath while I waited for his response.

"It'll involve following the trail," Cass said. "That depends how far back it goes. And…if he didn't leave a trail, I might have to go in and look at what he's been looking at. Do you have a problem with that?"

"Not at all," I said little too quickly. "I don't like people fucking with my business. It's my livelihood and that of the people who work for me." Never mind that I used to have as much money as people like Fairfield. The restaurant wasn't in danger of going under, but I still didn't want anyone fucking with it.

"Consider it done," he said. As if there was

nothing more to it than that. Even I knew it'd take him hours to do what he suggested. If not days.

Assuming it was even possible. He'd have to be good to get past Fairfield's security. I had a feeling I hadn't guessed incorrectly. Cass could do this. It would just take time.

"Thank you. I appreciate you." I handed him my plate when he started to pack up everything after we'd finished eating.

"Of course." He dumped all the dishes in the sink and turned around to lean against the counter. "I'm not sure there's anything I wouldn't do for you, Harlow." His eyes were darker, his gaze drifting up and down my body before settling on my face. It gave the impression he was memorizing every inch of me.

I hated myself even more. I knew that about him and I took advantage. I should tell him to forget about all of it and get the hell out of here right now. Run away and never look back. Take out a restraining order against myself so I wouldn't be tempted to go anywhere near him.

For some reason, my feet refused to move except to stand and walk over to him. The kitchen was so small, it only took a couple of steps until we were almost standing chest to chest.

"You're too sweet and too good for me," I said

softly. "You should find yourself a nice girl. Someone who will treat you right." Someone who wouldn't look at him and lie right to his face. Someone who wouldn't use him to plan a brutal killing.

He raised one hand slowly, brushed it past my cheek and over my hair. He grabbed a fist full and wound it around his fingers.

Holding me there, he brought his face closer to mine, close enough to swallow my gasp of surprise.

"I don't want a nice girl," he whispered. "I want a woman who knows what she wants."

What I knew right then was that my panties were ruined. This was a side of him I hadn't expected, but I liked it. He wasn't holding back now. I didn't want him to. I wanted everything he had to give to me. And then some.

"Do you?" I whispered back.

He turned his head to the side, regarding me before slowly swiveling it back the other way.

"You know what, you're right," he said. "I want a woman who knows what *I* want. Who's ready and willing to do what I tell her."

"What do you want?" I asked, meeting his gaze straight on. My heart raced, hoping I was picking up on the right vibe here. The whole being sweet thing was only one aspect of Cassius Titmus. Now it was time to let the darker side of him shine. The dominant side.

He proved me right a moment later. He tightened his grip on my hair and walked me backwards toward his bedroom. All the way to his bed, stopping when the back of my legs hit the mattress.

"I want you to lie down and put your arms over your head," he growled. He pressed me down onto my back and walked over to a set of drawers on one side of the bed. He slid one open and pulled out a length of purple rope. "Take your clothes off first."

I looked over to him. "And if I don't?"

This was a game, we just needed to establish the rules.

He wrapped the ends of the rope around his fingers and knelt on the side of the bed. "Then I'll cut them off you." The words were punctuated by hair falling over his eye. He pushed it back with the back of his hand, a bashful expression crossing his face. Rueful that the universe was reminding him that he was awkward, even when he was trying to be assertive.

My eyes on his, I undid the front of my skinny jeans and pushed them down my hips. I had to sit up to unlace my boots and toe them off. I kicked my jeans off onto the floor and grabbed the hem of my shirt.

Slowly, I pulled it up over my head and tossed it aside.

Just as slowly, I lay back and put my hands up over my head, lying in the middle of his bed in only my bra and panties.

His Adam's apple bobbed, front of his pants tenting as his erection grew.

"Good girl." He moved over closer, looping the smooth rope around my wrists and tying the other end to the headboard. Secure, but nothing I couldn't pull myself out of if I needed to.

He had to have known that. If I could flip him, then I could deal with him in this situation if I needed to. At the same time, it gave him a feeling of dominance; I saw that in his eyes.

"You like that? Being called a good girl." He sat beside me, his knees bent under him.

I hummed my agreement.

"Good, you can call me sir." He leaned down to my neck and traced a line from just under my ear to my throat, with his tongue.

I shivered. His touch was light, but sent a jolt right down to my core.

Slowly, he traced a line the opposite way, across to my other ear. He nibbled on the lobe before placing a hand beside my face and kissing my mouth. He tasted of taco, beer and something else I couldn't quite place. Something uniquely Cass. Whatever it was, I wanted more.

He traced the seam of my lips with his tongue, then moved down my cheek, my chin, my throat. He kissed his way down my chest and stomach

"I want to taste your pussy," he said.

"Yes, sir," I whispered. My panties were drenched by now. If I was any wetter, I'd start to trickle down my own thighs.

"Fuck," he whispered.

I sensed this was a fantasy he held for a long time. One that never happened for him. Not until now. It took someone to look past the awkward geek to see underneath. He was a man with needs, wants and from the look of the front of his pants, a decent-sized cock.

He gripped the waistband of my panties and slowly slid them down as if revealing a present on Christmas morning. Hoping he'd find what he asked Santa for, but hardly daring to believe it would be possible.

Judging by the widening of his eyes, he found exactly what he was wishing for. Neatly trimmed curls and a wet pussy.

He placed my panties aside as if they were a sacred object and parted my knees with his thighs.

"Did I do this?" He ran his thumb down my

pussy, from my clit to my entrance. "Are you this wet for me?"

"Yes, sir," I said again.

I barely finished speaking, when he pushed two fingers inside me. "You don't want me to be gentle." He didn't phrase it as a question, but it wasn't an assumption either.

"I can take it however you give it," I said. After a moment I added, "Sir."

He pushed his fingers in deeper, all the way up to the knuckle, then lowered his face and inhaled deeply again.

"You smell better than..." He shook his head, apparently unable to think of a comparison.

"Tacos?" I offered.

He looked up at me and grinned, showing those couple of crooked teeth. "Much better than tacos. Maybe even better than your meatballs."

I bit back a response to that. It was probably better if he didn't know how close he was to the truth.

He didn't seem to notice my internal struggle. His fingers still deep inside me, he tasted me with the tip of his tongue.

"No offense to your cooking, but you taste better." He glanced up at me, then started to lap at me while driving his fingers into me, over and over.

I had no answer for that. Nothing except to arch my back and push myself harder against his mouth. I wanted to touch my nipples, but I was still in my bra and with my hands bound above my head. The torture was sweet.

"Are you close?" he said between licks.

"So close," I panted.

"I want to see you come," he said. "I want to see you come while you're tied to my bed." He groaned at his own words. His cock must have been straining the seams of his pants, threatening to shred them.

"Yes, sir," I said breathlessly. I wanted that too. Not just because it was an orgasm, because this was his fantasy and I wanted it to be what he hoped. Better than he hoped.

He swallowed hard and went on working me with his tongue and fingers, pushing me toward an orgasm that had me crying out his name. Enveloped by a wave of warmth and pleasure. The heady rush of release that darkened my vision and made me see stars.

He went on working me until my flesh was too sensitive and I had to draw back a little.

"That was perfect." He crawled up until we were face-to-face again before pressing his mouth to mine, letting me taste myself on his lips. "You come nicely."

He kissed me again before reaching for the rope and untying it.

"You don't want to…" I started to say.

"Next time," he said. "This time I just wanted you to feel good."

"I did," I said. Except for the return of the guilt at lying to him. I trusted him to tie me up, but what reason have I given him to trust me?

CHAPTER 15

HARLOW

"What's he doing in there?" Erin looked over my shoulder in the direction of my office.

"Ensuring our online security," I said. At least I didn't have to lie to her about that.

"He's cute." She slid me a sly look. "I guess you took our advice and gave him a chance."

"I might have." I checked to make sure we had enough tomatoes for the next couple of days.

While trying not to look like I was looking at Cass.

While looking at Cass in the corner of my eye.

"Come on, give me something here." She gave me an 'out with it' gesture with her fingers.

I handed her an overripe tomato.

"Is this for throwing at you because you're not

giving me all the juicy details?" She threw it up in the air, caught it and made a face when it squelched. Hand covered in tomato juice and seeds, she tossed it into the trash.

I snorted softly. "I think that's what they call instant karma."

She glanced over at me as she washed her hands. "I want you to be happy, is that so bad? You took care of me when I needed it; I want to return the favor."

"You want to catch up on the gossip," I told her.

She grinned and swiped her hands on a towel. "Maybe a little. There's nothing wrong with harmless gossip. Besides, I'm only interested because I care about you. You and him are adorable together."

"We're just friends," I insisted. "I should go check on him."

"He's probably due for a top up on his milkshake," she said, as if the drink was dirty in some way. "If the office door is closed, we won't come a knockin'."

"I'm starting to rethink that apprenticeship," I said, giving her the eye before I filled up a milkshake glass with chocolate milkshake and slid a straw into it.

She laughed. "I know you love me. Make sure he's good to you. Otherwise he'll have me to deal with."

"I'm sure that will put the fear of God into him," I said sarcastically.

She was adorable, but if he needed to be dealt with, I could do it myself. I was almost certain it wouldn't come to that. So far, he hadn't given me any reason to think I needed to be violent with him. Unless it involved mutual pleasure.

I briefly wondered how he felt about paddles.

Shaking my head at her, and a little bit at myself, I carried the drink over to the office, placed it on the desk beside Cass and picked up the glass he'd emptied.

"Perfect timing." He looked up at me and smiled, apparently oblivious to the fact one of his lenses was completely obscured by his hair. "I was feeling thirsty." He leaned over and sucked on the straw.

I couldn't help remembering the way his mouth felt on my pussy. The way he'd made me come so hard. The feel of the shibari rope against my skin. Would he do more with the smooth rope than tie my wrists? Would I let him? The amount of control I'd have to give up to let him tie all of me made me want to squirm in both an arousing and an uncomfortable way at the same time. That might be something we could work up to.

One thing I was sure of: there was a lot more to Cassius Titmus than he let on. I was looking forward to digging down deeper. Between him and Boner, I was being spoiled for orgasms. At some point, I'd have to tell them about each other. Outside of hunting predators, I didn't do sneaking around. Or anything that might be perceived as cheating. If anything more than friendship developed between me and either of them, or Archer, everyone would know and understand what was going on. If they wanted to walk away, that was their choice.

As if thinking about him conjured him out of thin air, Boner walked in the front door of the restaurant, whistling a tune that sounded like the Ed Sheeran song, "Azizam."

"Morning, love," he said in his usual chipper voice. "This all looks very intense. Friend of yours?" He waved a hand between me and Cass before kissing my cheek.

"Yes, he is," I said. "Cassius Titmus, Edward Bonegard."

"Call me Boner," Boner said. After a beat he added, "Does anyone call you Tits?"

"No," Cass said. As if he remembered to be self-conscious, he pushed his hair off his face and his glasses back up his nose.

"Shame," Boner said, tucking his hands into his pockets. "Still, any friend of Harlow is a friend of mine."

He looked over at me and raised an eyebrow questioningly. Clearly wanting to know if Cass was the person I said could look into Granger Fairfield.

I responded with a tight nod. "Cass is looking into the security of my computer system," I said. "He's very good with computers."

"Is that so?" Boner took a hand out of his pocket and rubbed his chin. "Maybe he can look at mine when he's done with yours. A bloke can never be too careful."

"I'd be happy to," Cass said. He looked back at me. "So far, I can't find any sign you were hacked. I'm working on getting into Granger Fairfield's systems. Whoever set it up is good."

"This is where you say you're better, yeah?" Boner asked.

Cass looked over at him and smiled. "I don't want to brag."

"Why not? I do it all the time. Go on, tell us how good you are." Boner pointed a finger gun at him.

A blush crept up Cass' cheeks. "I'm very good. I haven't met a system I couldn't hack."

"There you go." Boner gave him a quick, light clap. "Felt good, didn't it?"

"I... Yeah, it did," Cass admitted. Looking like he'd reached his limit of the amount of time he could talk about himself, he picked up the milkshake and gave the straw a good suck.

"I like this guy," Boner said.

"Me too," I said.

"As much as you like me?" Boner cocked his head and he might have even fluttered his eyelashes.

Cass was watching us both, his eyes wide, straw pressed against his lower lip.

"Maybe more," I said, deliberately baiting Boner. He deserved it for putting me on the spot like that.

He straightened his head and frowned, then broke into a smile.

"You had me going for a while there, love. Lucky for all concerned, I don't mind sharing." He gave Cass a wink.

"I…" Cass started to say. He jerked his gaze back to the screen. "I'm in. Now I just need to figure out what I'm looking for."

I gave Boner a warning look before saying, "Anything that looks suspicious." I jerked a thumb toward Boner. "Apart from this guy. I know about him already."

Boner pretended to be outraged. "Did you just refer to me as suspicious?"

"How do I put this nicely…" I teased.

He huffed and tossed his head. "I'm starting to think you know me too well."

"Maybe you're just obvious?" I offered.

"Cass, do I look suspicious?" Boner asked.

Cass gave him a sideways look, but didn't respond.

"That's not a no," I said.

"It's not a yes either," Boner pointed out. He looked like he was about ready to strut like a rooster. The man wasn't short on ego, that was for sure.

I couldn't help liking that about him. He knew who he was and wasn't shy about expressing it. At the same time, he managed to be just this side of arrogant. Lucky for both of us, because I didn't do arrogant. Arrogant men were usually on the receiving end of a nice, sharp blade. Or a box filled with water. Or whatever other method I used to dispose of them. Sometimes I liked simplicity and sometimes I liked to challenge myself. It depended on the monster and my mood. Some of them didn't deserve to die too slowly.

"Um, Harlow?" Cass' voice was small, his eyes fixed on the screen.

My stomach dropped.

I didn't want to look, but my gaze went straight to the images he'd found.

"Fuck." I'd never *not* felt sick seeing things like this. This was the very worst of humanity. The deepest evil I could ever conceive of. And these weren't even the worst I'd seen.

"Excuse me." Cass' face had turned a shade of green. He flew up out of the chair, rushed past us and disappeared into the restroom. The sound of him throwing up the contents of his stomach was audible.

My stomach threatened to do the same, forcing me to swallow hard. I could deal with killing and dismembering a man, but this stuff was a whole different story. If the day came when I didn't feel sick or flinch at the sight of it, that was the day I'd know I lost my humanity. When I lost that, I wouldn't be able to trust my own judgement. What I'd do then, I didn't know, so I clung to my sanity as hard as I could. Focusing on monsters who deserved our kind of justice served to them. Reminding myself why I was doing this in the first place. For the innocent of the world. So they wouldn't end up on someone's hard drive. So they could live their lives and grow up the way they were supposed to.

"Can relate." Boner reached over and closed the laptop, his face dark with fury. "This is the guy."

"One of them," I agreed. "I think we can agree Archer's information on him is good."

"Yes," Boner said softly, barely containing his rage. If Fairfield was in front of him right now, he'd rip his balls off with his bare hands and make him eat them.

Honestly, I wouldn't try to stop him. I'd hold Fairfield down and let him do it. Perhaps while driving a blunt nail into his eyes, one at a time. Deep enough to hurt like a bitch, but not enough to kill him.

"We need to get together with Archer and deal with him," I said softly. "The sooner the better."

"Right. We'll need to look into his security and figure out where he's vulnerable. Then hit him there hard." He seemed to be thinking it over, making plans in his head.

"Who are you hitting?" I didn't know Cass returned until he was standing right behind us, staring at us like we were a pair of ghosts. "What's going on?" He looked deathly pale. "We should tell the cops."

"The cops can't touch people like Granger Fairfield," I said.

Cass frowned at me, his thoughts almost visibly turning around in his mind.

"That's why you wanted me to look into his computer, isn't it? Because you plan to touch him yourselves." He looked to the closed computer and back to us, clearly trying to work out who was the enemy here. Granger Fairfield or us.

"Touch is gentle compared to what he's got coming to him," Boner said unapologetically. "Him and people like him. That right there." He gestured to the laptop, "That's what people like him do. And people like us, Harlow and me, we don't let them get away with it."

I winced, hoping like hell he wasn't saying too much to someone who might run right to the police and tell them everything. I was acutely aware that we couldn't let Cass do that. Too much was at stake. I also, desperately didn't want him to *become* steak. None of this was his fault.

I should have kept him out of it.

Cass rubbed his forehead with his fingertips before adjusting his glasses with his thumb. "What do you want me to do?"

CHAPTER 16
BONER

"You shouldn't—" Harlow started.

"He's already involved," I said, anticipating what she was going to say. Should I have run my mouth off when Cass asked what was going on? To be honest, I knew what I was doing. The moment he saw those photos, he was in it up to his eyeballs. He had two choices, join us or *try* to walk away.

Yeah, we couldn't have risked him walking away. Even now, whether or not I trusted him, his involvement was still a big question mark.

He was clearly smitten with Harlow, but now that he knew what she was really like? That could disappear down the toilet faster than you can say flush.

Hell, knowing the real her changed everything for me. That first night with her was incredible, but seeing her on the fire escape outside Carl's apartment? Knowing why she was there? It made her a million times hotter than she already was.

Yeah, I was also smitten. Sue me.

"Maybe we should sit down." Harlow pushed the laptop to the side and sat on the desk.

Cass, who was still looking like a stunned sardine, needed a shove from me to flop into one of the chairs. That gave me room to close the door and lean against it. Barely. The office was the size of a closet.

"You knew what he was doing?" Cass asked carefully. Evidently reality was starting to seep back in. "That was why you wanted me here."

"We suspected," Harlow agreed. "We had to be sure. We knew there was a chance you'd see what you saw." She ran a hand over the back of her hair and tugged at her ponytail.

"We set you up," I said bluntly. There was no point apologizing for it. This whole thing was bigger than any of us.

"*I* set you up," Harlow said softly.

"It wasn't only you, love," I told her. "I was well aware whoever you asked to help would get caught up in it. We all understood that." I decided not to bring Archer's name into it yet. Cass had no idea a third person was involved. It would be better to keep it that way for now.

"Yes, but it was me who brought him into it," Harlow said. "I'm sorry, Cass I—"

"I want to help," Cass said. He shook his head slowly, the front of his hair falling over his face before he pushed it back. "However all of this went down, it went down. What I saw, I can't unsee, but I can do something about it. Right?" He looked from Harlow to me and back again.

"You don't know what you're asking," she said.

"Yes, he does." I eyed him carefully. "He knows exactly what he's asking, but what I don't know is why. Why do you want to help?"

"Why do you?" Cass shot back at me.

Knowing he could just as easily end up being cubed, slid onto a skewer and barbecued, I told him my story in as few words as I could. Then glanced at Harlow before telling him about her sister.

"You've seen mine, show me yours," I said. "You or someone close to you?" Yeah, that was direct, but I'd been the same with him. If he was going to join our little crusade, then he was going to have to give us something.

"My younger brother," Cass said slowly, like he'd prefer to have his teeth pulled one by one. "He took his own life because of it." He didn't go into detail and I didn't ask.

Harlow slid off the desk and knelt in front of him, her hands on his knees. "I'm so sorry. If I'd had any idea, I never would have asked you to get involved."

I squinted at Cass. "You didn't have to," I said. "You only had to give him Granger Fairfield's name. He already knew."

Cass swallowed. "I had my suspicions. He was friends with Fairfield's son. He had a sleepover there one night. When he came back..." He pressed his eyes shut. "He was different. He refused to talk about it. He shut down. A few weeks later he..." His voice broke on the last couple of words.

"Fuck," Harlow whispered. "I'm so sorry. How old was he?"

"He was seventeen," Cass said, dropping his eyes.

"You never spoke to the cops about it?" I asked.

Cass didn't respond at first. He kept his head down for a minute or two. Finally, he looked up and over at me.

"And tell them what? I had no proof. Now we have proof. But you're right. They won't touch him. He's too powerful." He looked back at Harlow. "Is this what you do? You hunt down people like him and you...what? Kill them?" His voice was higher on the last couple of words.

"Yes," she said. "We make sure they can't do it to anyone else."

"You've never been caught." It wasn't a question. Obviously she hadn't or she wouldn't be here right now.

She smiled slightly. "I'm good at...covering my tracks."

"So am I," I said. I leaned back against the door and crossed my arms like the cocky fuck I was.

"This is insane," Cass said to himself.

"The necessity is insane," I agreed. "No one should be so powerful they get away with anything and everything. The law can't do anything about it, but we can and we do. In a perfect world, we wouldn't need to."

"In a perfect world, people like Granger Fairfield wouldn't exist," Harlow said darkly. "Fucked up monsters. But they do, and I refuse to let them continue. He murdered my sister and I can't forgive that. I won't let him keep doing it. I can't."

"He'll get a nasty, painful, preferably slow death," I assured her, trying to contain how turned on I was by her passion.

"What was your brother's name?" I was a big believer in knowing all the names, so they wouldn't be forgotten. It was my way of honoring the people we'd lost.

Admittedly, in this case, I wanted to observe Cass's sincerity. Call it risk assessment if you like. If I was going to turn my back on him, I wanted to know I wouldn't find a knife in it.

That kind of information was somewhat important.

"Augustus," Cass said. "My parents had a thing for ancient Rome. My older brother's name is Julius." He made a face and then added, "He goes by Jules."

"Thank fuck they didn't name any of you Nero," I said. "Or Caligula. Screwy in the head, both of them." I made a screwing motion in the air with my finger. As in, driving one into a piece of wood with a screwdriver, not the fucking kind of screwing.

Although, they were similar, now I thought about it.

"Yeah it could have been worse," Cass agreed. "So, what do we do now? I want to help." He pressed his lips into a line so tight they went white. "I've waited long enough for justice for Auggie."

"We need to figure out where Fairfield is and how to get at him," Harlow said. "When and where he's the most vulnerable." A fire burned in her eyes, like she was ready to burn the world down on behalf of her sister.

Totally fair. If I had a sister and anyone did to her what they'd done to Lettie, I'd burn the whole fucking universe down. Same if anyone tried to touch a hair on Harlow's head. It wouldn't be the first time I'd cut off hands. It wouldn't even be the first time I slapped them across the face with their own fingers.

That was funnier than it should have been.

No, it was just fucking funny.

You should have seen the expression on the guy's face. Somewhere right between offended and in a shit ton of pain. It was a thing of beauty.

"I can get a hold of his schedule," Cass said. "That shouldn't be too difficult. Taking down his security system long enough for us to get in and out is doable." His mind was turning over with thoughts and plans, I could see that in his eyes. Although, I suspected his ideas were straight out of a Hollywood movie. I liked the guy, but he had a lot to learn. He better learn it quickly.

"You won't be going in with me," Harlow told him.

"Us," I corrected. "I'm not sitting out."

She looked like she was about to start arguing with me, but closed her eyes and exhaled slowly.

"We need to make a plan," she said. "Then we can work out who's doing what."

"I can get behind that," I said. Of course, I was going to make sure I was as involved as possible. I'd be happy to go in alone if need be. Whatever it took to get the job done.

She raised an eyebrow at me in justified suspicion. Yes, I was up to something, why else would I back down so quickly?

We both knew what I was up to. I wasn't going to be left out. Never let it be said that I wasn't a stubborn prick.

"Okay, let's get that schedule first," she said. "Then we can go from there." She rose and moved the laptop back into the center of the desk. "You think you can find it without seeing anything else?" From the way her hand pressed down on the lid of the laptop, she wasn't going to open it again if it meant confronting Cass with more.

"It's probably publicly available," Cass said. "I won't need to go back into that…area." He rolled the chair closer. "He'll notice if we delete all of that, won't he?" He sounded regretful.

"He might," she agreed. "Once we deal with him, we can delete it. Or make sure the cops find it. They'll be looking for a motive. We can give them one. Let them see what he was really like. Hopefully that will give everyone some closure."

I'd like to think the police wouldn't look quite as hard for his killer once they realized he got exactly what he deserved. Unfortunately, every cop I'd ever met was dogged about doing their duty. Even if they completely agreed with what we did, they'd keep looking until the trail went stone cold. Which would be quick, because we were, after all, good at covering our asses.

Sometimes I felt sorry for them. I thought about joining the force when I was younger. Once I saw how tied their hands were by the law, I abandoned the idea. Having to abide by the rules would have driven me crazy.

If I wore a hat, I'd take it off to them. Instead, I occasionally threw them a proverbial bone. Making sure they got leads to find the kind of people who deserved to be locked away, rather than dead.

I'm a vigilante, not an asshole.

"Right." Cass waited until Harlow stepped aside before easing the laptop open and waking up the screen. He closed out of the files he'd hacked into and tapped at the keyboard, looking for Fairfield's schedule.

I watched Harlow watching him, her expression difficult to read. She really didn't want to drag him into this, but he was in it. I understood her apprehension. Not just bringing a guy like this into the craziness, but working with him, me and Archer as well.

And dating us. Yeah, I knew Archer had a thing for her too. This whole situation could easily become complicated, and people like us didn't like complications.

As for me, I couldn't drag myself away from her if I wanted to. I could very easily fall for this woman. I'd die for her. I'd definitely kill for her. I'd drive a knife into Cass' neck right now if he showed any sign of not being on our side. If he didn't think I'd watch him closely, then he needed to think again.

People like me, we didn't survive by being naïve. We survived by being untrusting, suspicious pricks. Something I definitely intended to continue being for as long as I lived.

"Okay, I'm in," Cass said. He leaned in closer to the screen. "This lists every place he'll be for the next eight weeks." After a few moments of reading, he whispered, "Fuck…"

CHAPTER 17

HARLOW

"Have you ever been down here?" Archer glanced over at me before stepping carefully over a crack in the brick flooring. His voice echoed slightly in the tunnel, eerily sending it back to us.

"Not here specifically," I whispered. "And not for a long time."

"You okay?" he asked. "Five percent of the population of the country suffers from claustrophobia. If you want to turn back, we can."

Of course he'd know a figure like that. Honestly, I was surprised it wasn't higher.

"I'm fine," I said quickly. "These tunnels are creepy, that's all." Not to mention an entire city rested over them. They'd lasted this long, but that didn't mean they wouldn't choose today to collapse.

"I like them," he said, running his hand along the wall beside him. "It's peaceful in here. Almost like the rest of the world doesn't exist anymore. It could end and we'd still be here, safe."

"Safe until we ran out of oxygen," I said. "Which would take…" I guessed he'd know the answer to that too. Or at least be able to quote some study or Internet meme that may or may not be factual.

"We have enough time to get to the surface and see all the billionaires get on their secret spaceship and leave," he said. "If we're lucky, we might get on it too."

I couldn't tell if he was serious or not. "I don't think I want to be on a spaceship with a bunch of billionaires. I'll take my chances with the zombies."

"It's all fun and games until you become one." He flashed me a smile. "Have you ever eaten brains?"

"As a matter of fact," I said slowly. Not human brains. I'd cooked one once, using the same recipe as I would for pig brains, but knowing what horrible things went through his mind when he was alive, I didn't want to put that in my mouth. I served it to my next target though, with no regrets. He seemed to enjoy it. Until I sliced into his stomach to remove it again. He didn't enjoy that nearly as much.

"They were nice," I added. "But not nice enough to

make it my whole life. I'd probably make a terrible zombie anyway."

"I think you'd be a gorgeous zombie," he said. "But it's not your brains I want to eat."

The pulse in my pussy throbbed, but I told her to settle. This was not the time. Whether or not it was the place was debatable.

We reached the end of the tunnel, a locked door blocking the way out.

Archer reached into his pocket and pulled out a lock picking device.

"Where does this lead?" I asked.

"Into the hotel Contessa," he said as he picked the lock and opened the door slowly.

"The other way leads to Grand Central Station." He gestured one way down the tunnel he'd opened, then the other. "These were used back in the day for people to travel between them. Right now though, we're going to the hotel. One of their clients is someone I thought you should meet."

"And by 'meet,' you mean 'help you kill,'" I said. He'd implied that when he told me where to meet him and to dress in black.

"Exactly," he said. "This guy is particularly nasty. Just your cup of tea."

"Oh?" I followed him into the new tunnel.

"He doesn't get his hands dirty, directly," Archer

said. "He arranges for his customers to get what they want, per their particular tastes and requirements. He calls himself the Concierge of Pleasure." He curled his lip in disgust. "More like the Concierge of Depravity."

"I've heard of him," I said. "I haven't been able to find out who he really is." I was impressed Archer had.

"His name is Wolfgang Taylor-Francis," Archer said. "No doubt you've heard of him."

I frowned. "He's some kind of Wall Street trader. Friends with a bunch of politicians and people like that. Didn't he speak out about government transparency or something?"

"Exactly." Archer slipped the lock picking tool back into his pocket. "On the surface, he's squeaky clean. A nice guy." He used air quotes. "The kind of man I'd vote for if he ran for office. But that's just on the surface. Underneath that, he's a snake. Corrupt as fuck. He uses his reputation to get into places and slide back out of them again, untouched."

"What the fuck?" I whispered. "I have to admit, I had no idea. Are you sure?"

"As sure as I am that I'm almost finished crocheting a rabbit. I'll have to show you sometime." When I gave him a funny look, he shrugged. "It helps me relax. I can't be about death all of the time."

"I hear you," I said. "For me, it's cooking. Creating a dish from scratch is very satisfying."

"It's the little things that help to keep us grounded," he said. "If we didn't have that, we'd lose ourselves. According to research, people like us often create intricate fantasies and then try to live them out. Crocheting helps to remind me of what's real."

"Most of my intricate fantasies are about finding everyone who hurt my sister," I said.

Others involved paddles and orgasms.

"What will you do after that?" Archer took my hand and we walked slowly down the tunnel toward the Contessa. "When they're all dead. Have you thought about that?"

His hand was firm and warm in mine, reassuring. Some simplicity amid all of the complications.

"Not really," I admitted. "Part of me doesn't think it's possible to find them all. What if they're already dead? What if I never find them?" I exhaled, hard and frustrated.

"Even if I find them all, there's other monsters out there. How can I stop, knowing what I know? Knowing that if I let them slide, they'll hurt more innocent people?"

He squeezed my hand. "Yeah, same. There's always going to be someone. While there's even one of them left, I can't let it go."

"Exactly," I whispered. "There's always going to be another monster waiting in the shadows." Until they were all dead or I was, I'd keep doing what I was doing.

"You're beautiful when you're vengeful," Archer said.

We reached another door, also locked from this side. He pulled out the lock pick and worked this one open.

The second door led into a room that was pitch black except for the light from our phones. It seemed to be a storeroom forgotten by time. To one side, a handful of chairs were covered in dust. What looked like paintings leaned against the opposite wall, just as dusty.

"How did you know about this place?" I asked.

"I have my ways," was all he said. "There should be a stairway up ahead that leads into the back corridors of the hotel. From there, we need to take the service elevator."

"I feel like a kid," I said.

"You crept around in hotels at two o'clock in the morning as a kid?" He moved his phone around, looking for the stairs.

"You'd be surprised," I said dryly. "But no, my sister and I used to play hide and seek. The basement of our building was our favorite place. It was dark, creepy and full of stuff. Sometimes, we'd go down there with a flashlight and a book and curl up for hours and read."

"You have good memories of your sister?" He shone the phone toward me before realizing the light was in my eyes and shining it away. "Sorry."

"I have the best memories." I blinked a couple of times to recover my vision. "Sometimes we'd fight, like siblings do, but mostly we got along. What they did to her— I feel like I let her down."

I was the big sister, it was my job to make sure nothing happened to her. Mine and my parents', but when they couldn't, I should have. I should have been able to protect her.

Archer pulled me over to him and drew me closer, his hand slipping out of mine and going to my lower back.

"You did not let her down," he whispered fiercely, his mouth an inch from mine. "They did. Your father. Those men. *They* did that. If you knew what they were planning, you never would have let them near her. You would have done *everything* you could to stop them. Anything."

"How could I not know?" I argued, without heat or force. "How can I have missed the signs that something was going on? I look at it now and it seemed…

obvious. My father was being squirrelly. I should have guessed, I should have known."

"Do. Not. Blame. Yourself." He was insistent. His breath brushed my lips, body pressed against mine. "Men like that, they wouldn't have let you get in their way. They would have killed you or you would have ended up like her. Used and then thrown away." He sounded stabby.

"She and I could have run away," I said. He was right, I knew that. I couldn't have stopped it any more than I could stop the sun from rising. That wouldn't lessen the guilt that plagued me. It wouldn't help me sleep better at night. It wouldn't stop me from dreaming about her, or the deaths of her tormentors I found and dealt with.

"You could have tried," he said. "That would have ended one of two ways. One, they find you and everything happens the way they wanted it to happen. Or two, you spend the rest of your life looking over your shoulder. Maybe trying to get them before they get you."

"I'd take the second one if it meant my sister was still alive," I said without hesitation. It seemed like a small price to pay.

"You might not have had a choice," he said. "You don't know what might have gone down. None of us do. We can make the present and the future the best we can, that's it. I know it sucks, but would she want you to blame yourself?"

"Of course not," I said immediately. "She would have wanted…" I sighed out my nose. "Me to get on with my life and put her behind me. I can't do that either. I can't put her memory to rest until they're all gone to Hades."

Sometimes I wondered if eternal torture was enough, but it wasn't for me to decide. Nor did I really believe in it. If I could choose, I'd prefer they'd get reincarnated as something nasty and short-lived, like a mosquito. Or a flea. Maybe a turkey that makes people happy by ending up Christmas dinner.

That was more poetic justice than they deserved.

"Then we'll do what we can to take them down," he said. "You, me, that Boner guy and your computer geek friend. Was he sure about what he saw on the schedule?"

"I saw it too," I said. "Granger Fairfield will be in the city for two nights a week from now. That's when we'll deal with him."

Archer nodded slowly. "Okay. Let's go and deal with Taylor-Francis first. Then we can think about Fairfield." He brushed his lips over mine, soft at first but then deeper and more demanding. Hungry like he'd been holding back for the longest time.

I found myself kissing him back, letting his

tongue slide between my lips and tasting my mouth. Then we were both stepping back, catching our breath and turning in the direction of the stairs.

"Let's end this asshole," I said.

"That's my girl," Archer said approvingly. "One dead asshole, coming up."

He gripped my hand again and we headed toward the stairs.

The corridor was silent except for the creak and groan of water passing through the pipes, and the buzz of electricity. Can lights illuminated the ceiling every few feet with a dim, cool glow.

Behind one of the doors, someone spoke in a low voice. They got louder for a few moments before dropping down again. Talking on their phone while pacing back and forth, unless I missed my guess.

The voice got closer again. "That's it baby, touch that clit for me. I want to hear you come…" His voice faded again.

I glanced over at Archer and grinned, even though he wouldn't see my mouth behind the mask I'd just pulled on. Two o'clock in the morning was as good a time as any for phone sex.

Archer shrugged and led the way to room six-six-nine. Out of his pocket, he pulled a card.

"Universal key," he whispered.

"I need one," I whispered back. Being able to get into any hotel room in the city would be useful.

He swiped it over the reader until it flashed green and clicked. Pushing his shoulder into it, he opened the heavy door slowly.

I followed him in, careful not to let it slam behind us. A door this heavy would wake the dead, much less Wolfgang Taylor-Francis.

The curtains were open, letting in the light from the city. Illuminating the entryway and stand that held a suitcase with the initials WTF embossed on them. Confirming we were in the right room.

Walking lightly on the carpeted floor, we made our way to the bedroom. A man lay half under the covers. A woman beside him.

She was naked, curled up like she wanted to make herself smaller. Her arms wrapped around her knees, her eyes wide open, staring at us. Her eyes were huge in her dainty face. Skin a pale contrast to dark hair.

Shit.

She lifted her head, but dropped it back down and curled up tighter. It was then I saw the bruises and the shine in her eyes. The fear, but not of us. She was terrified of the man who lay beside her. The marks he'd left on her body.

I held my hand out to her. She wouldn't want to see what we were about to do. She might have lain here night after night, wishing for it to happen, but the reality would haunt her. If I could save her from that, I would.

She glanced over her shoulder at the sleeping man before sliding out of bed and grabbing up something from the floor.

I was about to go for my knife when I saw her pulling on a dress, jamming it over her head and tugging it into place. She reached out and took my hand, squeezing it hard, her expression earnest, grateful.

I squeezed her hands back. She was young, no more than her early twenties. Familiar. His young wife or fiancée, unless I was mistaken.

She leaned forward and whispered in my ear, "Please, make it hurt." Before I could respond, she darted into the bathroom and closed the door behind her.

"I like her," I whispered.

"I don't like him." Archer had his knife out and pointing at Taylor-Francis. He pulled the sheets back from him and slid the blade right into the bottom of his foot.

Taylor-Francis woke with a squeal of pain that sounded like a pig.

"What the hell?" He jerked his foot away, sending blood spraying all over the white sheets. "Fuck. Fuck. Fuck." He drew his foot up and jammed his finger into the hole, making his hairy stomach bulge wider.

"Nice one," I told Archer.

Right in the arch of the asshole's foot. Now *that* was poetic.

"Thanks. I should have researched how long it takes to die from a stab wound to the foot." Archer sounded annoyed with himself.

"I don't know, but I have a feeling it's a long time," I said. Honestly, I was surprised he didn't have that knowledge on hand, but here we were.

"You're right," he said. "A stab to the stomach could take few hours. The foot would be much longer."

"What they hell are you talking about?" Taylor-Francis scrambled back up to the end of the bed, mouth hanging open. "What do you want? Do you want money? I can give you money. As much as you need. Just, please, don't hurt me."

I couldn't help noticing he didn't even look for his wife. I'd like to say I was surprised, but I wasn't. Men like him, they only looked out for themselves.

"I don't need money," I said. "I've got plenty."

"Then what do you want? I know people. Whatever you need, I can pull strings." He was becoming increasingly desperate, eyes frantic at the amount of blood drenching the bed.

"A nice slice of the groin, right through the femoral artery, works nicely," I said. "If you don't mind having your hand so close to a tiny penis."

Apparently his foot wasn't so bad anymore, because his hands flew up to cover his dick.

"Please," he begged. "I'll give you anything. *Anything.*" He glanced down, at least self-aware enough to be revolted as he pissed himself on his own fingers.

"See, that's the problem with people like you," Archer said, stalking closer. "You're okay with hurting women, but when it comes to yourself? You're a quivering bowl of Jell-O." He didn't attempt to mask the contempt in his voice.

"I don't…" Now Taylor-Francis glanced around. "It was an accident. Whatever she told you, I didn't mean it. I'll be more careful next time." But his expression was angry, not repentant. He'd convinced himself she'd brought us in somehow. If we took his word for it and left, he'd take it out on her. He'd probably kill her.

"No, you won't," Archer said. "If we walk out of here, you'll do the exact same things over and over. Sable doesn't deserve the things you did to her."

Of course he'd know her name. He would have researched her before we got here. Some of it might even be accurate. When it came to famous people, the Internet wasn't known for being a source of facts. Some ridiculous rumor was always circulating. Usually multiple.

"It was an accident," Taylor-Francis insisted. "She fell."

"Falling doesn't usually leave handprints," Archer pointed out. "I'd be willing to bet that in less than one percent of falls, handprints were involved. When they were, it was only because someone was trying to stop them from falling."

Taylor-Francis seized on that. "That's what happened. She tripped and I tried to save her."

"Do you usually catch people on their breasts?" I asked. I'd seen finger marks there.

"I have a theory," Archer said.

"If your theory is this guy is a lying fuck, I agree," I said.

"So do I, but that wasn't my theory," Archer said. "My theory is he has no heart. That's my hypothesis. My proposal is that I test this hypothesis by carving a hole in his chest and taking a look."

"No!" Taylor-Francis scrambled back so fast he fell

off the opposite side of the bed with a thud. Looking dazed, he clambered to his feet and pressed his back against the window. "Don't come any closer."

"What will you do, beat us to death with your tiny penis?" I asked. I was careful not to look at it. Life was traumatic enough without subjecting myself to a sight like that.

"I'll scream," he said, frantically looking for Sable, who was definitely not coming to his rescue. He tried to back up as Archer and I closed in on him.

"I usually prefer things to be less messy than this," I said, sighing at the bloody footprints on the carpet.

"They'll charge the cleaning fee to his credit card," Archer said. Then he lunged at Taylor-Francis, and driving the knife deep into his chest. His other hand went over the man's mouth, containing his cry of surprise and pain.

For a few long moments, they stood like that, until Taylor-Francis started to slide down the window and onto the floor.

I helped Archer to lower him and lay him out while he took his last, gurgling breaths.

Archer slid his knife free before making a series of incisions, carving through skin and muscle before he grunted. "Seems I was wrong."

Slicing carefully, he removed Taylor-Francis' heart from his chest cavity and held it up towards me.

"I like you, Harlow," he whispered, sounding shy behind his mask.

"That's so sweet." I reached behind me for a pillow, slid off the case and wrapped the heart up carefully. "I don't think anyone's given me an actual heart before."

"Yeah, well… He didn't need it anymore." Archer cleaned his knife on the side of the sheets and slipped it away. "We should get out of here."

"Good idea." The sun would be up in another hour or two. We needed to be long gone before then. Holding my gift carefully, I stood and headed over to the bathroom.

Just as I got there, Sable opened the door a crack. "Is he…"

"Yeah," I said softly. "Maybe give us an hour or two before you 'find' him. Have a long soak in the tub or something." She wouldn't have seen me smile, but hopefully she heard it in my voice.

"I will," she said, nodding vigorously. "Thank you. Is it wrong that I'm relieved?"

"Not at all," I assured her. Besides, if I thought it was wrong for her to feel good about his death, what did that say about me and Archer for doing it? "Maybe donate some of his money to a woman's shelter."

"Of course I will." She seemed to like that idea.

The next few days were going to be rough, but the police would find evidence that somebody stronger than her killed Taylor-Francis while she was in the bath. She was dainty, too small to carve his heart out.

I wished she didn't have to see him lying like that, but that was unavoidable. There was too much blood for us to sneak away with his body and not have people asking questions. Not to mention, it would be harder to find her innocent without proof of a crime she couldn't have committed. Blood was too easy to misconstrue.

I gave her a nod and opened the door, stepping out into the corridor, Archer right behind me.

"As romantic dates go, that was nice," I told him. "Thank you."

"It's true what the meme says." He took my elbow and led me back towards the stairs. "Women don't want flowers and chocolates, they want the hearts of their enemies and a cottage in the woods. I'll have to work on the second one."

"I don't need a cottage in the woods," I said with a laugh.

We hurried down into the darkness and through the tunnel that led back the way we came. Carefully wiping down door handles and banisters as we passed.

Finally, we reached the door we'd used to enter

the tunnels and quickly changed into the clothes we left in a bag beside it, stuffing our black outfits and masks inside in their place. By the time we were finished, we looked like two regular people, out for an early morning run. Me in lycra and a tank top. Him in a T-shirt and loose shorts.

Tossing the bag over his shoulder, Archer took my hand and we walked away just as the sound of sirens started approaching. No part of me was concerned. This was New York City. These sirens might not even be about Taylor-Francis. If they were, we'd be long gone before they arrived.

Instead of panicking, I smiled to myself. The world was a slightly better place than it was when the sun set last night.

"One down, how many more to go?" I asked. The adrenaline was still rushing through me. I wanted to take them all on at once.

"One that matters for now," Archer said. "Granger Fairfield."

CHAPTER 19

HARLOW

"We have a bit of a problem." Gina stuck her head into the kitchen and grimaced. "There's a customer out here who would like to speak to the chef."

"Did they say what about?" I washed and dried my hands before before tossing the towel into the laundry basket.

She spread her hands to either side in a shrug. "He doesn't seem happy." He must be bad if she was looking irritated. Gina Lopez was the cranky customer whisperer. Whatever problem people had, she always had a way of soothing things over. Almost always. Some people couldn't be placated.

They don't say customer service is difficult for nothing.

"Okay," I said with a sigh. "I have a few minutes."

I glanced back to make sure Erin was okay with me stepping out before I headed over to the table Gina indicated.

A man a couple of years older than me sat by himself near the window. He had a menu in his hands and a scowl on his face.

"Afternoon, is there a problem?" I asked. Might as well cut right to the chase.

"My brother told me about this place," he said, his gaze raking up my body until he finally found where my eyes were. "What's good?"

He insisted I come out here so he could ask me that? At least he wasn't a cop. Whatever his gripe was, he wasn't trying to pin anything on me.

"It's all good," I said easily. "Depends what you're in the mood for." I crossed my arms and regarded him. He was handsome enough in an arrogant sort of way. Wavy dark hair, three or four days of stubble on his chin. A piercing in his eyebrow above his right eye. For some reason, that one seemed bluer than the other. His left eye was more blue-green.

"What's the most popular dish?" He closed his menu and placed it on the table beside his fork.

"The spaghetti Bolognese," I said. "Made fresh every day." I was starting to regret the decision to leave Taylor-Francis' body back at the hotel. This guy could have used a heaping bowl of WTF, with a sprinkle of Parmesan cheese.

"What do you have that's not pasta?" He placed his forearms on the table, displaying skin covered in ink.

"You know this is an Italian restaurant, right?" I asked. "Pasta is kinda our thing. But we also have garlic bread, salad and risotto. The risotto is rice, not pasta." In case he didn't know.

"Salad," he echoed, his lip turned up in a sneer. "Do I look like a rabbit?"

"Rabbits can mate multiple times a day, so I'd say no, you don't," I said sweetly.

Archer would be proud of me for spouting off a fact like that. Although, he'd have a better idea of the exact numbers. As retorts went, it would do.

His sneer turned into a smirk. "Babe, if you think I can't fuck a bunch of times a day, you better think again."

"If you say so," I said. "I prefer a man who knows what he's doing once."

He snorted. "I bet you date the kind of guys who don't know where to find the clit."

I matched his snort. "You'd lose that bet. Now, what can I get you to eat?" Did we have any meatballs left from last time? I didn't think we did, unfortunately. Shame, I'd enjoy watching him eat, oblivious to what, or who, he was consuming.

"Jules, you made it." Cass stepped through the door, a smile on his face like he was actually pleased to see this clown.

"Of course I did, bro." Jules half-stood and reached out to shake his brother's hand. "I was just about to tell this chick what she can cook for me." He dropped back down into his chair.

"I'd tell you to make your own sandwich, but you can stay out of my kitchen." I accepted the side hug from Cass and let my lips linger over his when he kissed me.

"Seems like you didn't tell me everything." Jules glared at both of us.

I ignored him and said, "I have some ravioli I think you'll love, and I've been experimenting with flavors for a new kind of milkshake if you're game to try."

"That sounds perfect." Cass smiled softly. "Thank you." His cheeks turned pink, but he leaned in to press his nose to mine. "Jules, you should try her ravioli. It's so good."

I wanted to say Jules could stay the hell away from my *ravioli*, but I'd serve them both some pasta. "Two bowls of ravioli and a milkshake, coming up."

"You aren't still drinking that shit, are you?" This

time, Jules' lip curl was aimed at his brother. "I'll take water. I'm careful about what I put in my body."

Once again, I regretted not having any of Taylor-Francis in my fridge.

I gave Jules a smile and said, "Funny, me too." None of his body parts were going anywhere near mine, especially my pussy. How did a guy like Cass have an asshole for a brother? I assumed when nature gave out personalities, they gave Jules' portion to Cass.

"You say that now." Jules looked cocky, although I got the impression the previous part of our conversation sank in. The bit about his brother knowing where to find my clit.

"I'll go and fix your lunch." I kissed Cass' cheek, rolled my eyes at Jules and headed back into the kitchen.

"What was that about?" Gina whispered when I stepped back into the kitchen.

"Entitlement," I said. "Apparently that's Cass' brother."

"He's sorta hot." She peered past me, her head cocked as she appraised him.

"He's all yours," I said darkly.

I grabbed a couple of bowls and started to fill them with ravioli and sauce, while Erin made a milkshake. I was tempted to put more food in Cass' bowl than in Jules', but I decided not to be petty. The guy had the look of someone who'd take a photo and post it to social media to demonstrate my apparent imperfection. It was better not to give people like that any ammunition.

"Judging by the way he was looking at you, he doesn't know I exist." Gina picked up the bowls in one hand and the milkshake in the other and carried them over to the table.

I watched as both of them stabbed ravioli with their forks and brought them to their mouths, fully expecting Jules to spit his out or complain. Instead, he chewed and swallowed, and reluctantly shrugged a shoulder before continuing to eat.

One point to Harlow St. James. Two if you count my rabbit retort.

Three if you count the way Cass sounded like he was having an orgasm right now at the taste of his lunch.

If he kept doing that, he was going to make me ruin my panties. Not just because it sounded hot, but because I liked when people appreciated my cooking. What can I say, good taste is attractive.

Why did he ask his brother to meet him here though? He wanted justice for his other brother, but we were supposed to meet Archer and Boner once the lunch service was over. We had plans to make and things to decide. This was the best place to do it. No one would question us gathering here, and no one could listen in or watch us without me knowing.

At some point, I might let the guys see my apartment. I didn't think they'd be shocked by what they saw there, but at the same time it was still my sanctuary. Besides, Cass might not be ready to see my torture box. That was definitely something I'd have to work up to. The list of those was adding up.

I shook my head and went back to finishing the last few dishes for the lunch order, and preparing things for dinner.

"Are you okay?" Erin asked, shooting me a concerned look. "You seem tired today."

I glanced over to her and smiled. "I'm fine. I didn't get much sleep last night."

I got maybe an hour before I had to get back up and come in here. I made a mental note to plan more murders for a Monday, so I could sleep in on Tuesday. Of course, when a Thursday night was your only option, you had to take it. If we hadn't, Sable would have suffered for longer. Potentially much longer, depending on when another opportunity presented itself.

According to a quick search online, Sable Taylor-Francis was distraught at the death of her husband, and was helping police. They had no immediate suspects, but a long list of his enemies. A man like that wouldn't be mourned for long.

Of course, the same could be said about me. Sure, I was getting close to three attractive men, and Gina and Erin cared about me, but they were the closest I had to family. If anything happened to me, they'd find new jobs and crushes, and get on with their lives.

That thought was depressing. Just because serial killers were supposed to be loners, didn't mean I wanted to be one myself. A loner, that was. I had no issue with being a serial killer. Okay, maybe one issue. I was so good at covering my tracks, the police hadn't given me a fancy name. Nor had I given myself one.

What would I go with if I did? Everything I could think of seemed cliché to me. Or downright silly. Avenging Angel sounded fancy, but I doubted the police would use something so positive. More like the Monster of Meatballs. That definitely sat squarely in the silly category. So did the Butcher of Bolognese, although that did have a ring to it. Monster of Milkshakes? Also too silly.

"I need to learn how to do more, so you can go home and get some rest if you need to," Erin said. "That's what I'm here for, right?"

I patted her shoulder. "You will. I'll be okay. I'll

get some rest before the dinner service." More than likely, I wouldn't. Not with all the plans we had to make. What was it they say? Sleep is for the weak? I'd catch up with rest later.

She gave me a fierce look. "You better." She even shook her finger at me, as if she wasn't younger than me, and my employee.

I laughed. "Thank you for being sweet. I appreciate it. Now, shouldn't you be washing dishes?" I raised my eyebrows and gave her my best 'boss babe' expression. The one that said, 'I adore you, but get back to work.'

That earned me a sideways look, but she hurried over to stack dishes into the dishwasher and wash the pots. The definition of a never ending story. Some days it felt like we washed twenty plates, only to have another fifty turn up, needing to be scrubbed. That was a good thing, it kept the restaurant open, but I'd like to hire more staff some day. Another chef so I could take time off. Another server and someone who could just wash dishes. I'd have to sit down with my accountant and crunch some numbers.

I glanced out to the sitting area to see Jules' gaze on me. He seemed to be half-listening to whatever Cass was saying, the rest of his attention focused on trying to figure me out.

Good luck with that, I told him silently.

Like his brother, I was more complicated than I was at face value. With layers someone like him wouldn't be able to imagine, much less see. Let him look, let him dig, he wasn't going to find anything.

His eyes narrowed slowly as if he was reading my thoughts now. He lifted his chin and turned his face away, back to his brother. His posture relaxed, but something about him gave me chills.

CHAPTER 20
BONER

"Who's this clown?" I slipped into the chair beside Cass and jerked my head at the man he was sitting with. He looked like he got a strap-on stuck up his ass during a particularly vigorous session of anal. My advice? Make sure you use enough lube. Otherwise, you might end up looking like this guy.

"Who the fuck are you?" Grumpy-ass snarled. Which, I supposed, was a fair question. I had come at him pretty hard, figuratively speaking.

"Jules, this is Boner," Cass said, looking suitably embarrassed.

To be completely honest, I loved the way people looked when they said my nickname out loud. Until they got used to it, it was good for shits and giggles.

I reached over to offer my hand to Jules. "You're Cassius' brother. Tell me, do they call *you* Tits?"

Jules looked at my hand like if he touched it, it might set him on fire. I wished it could, because that would be an awesome party trick.

"No," he snapped. "What sort of name is Boner?"

I sat back and grinned, unbothered by his rejection of a perfectly civil handshake.

"That should be obvious. An awesome one."

"It's a nickname," Cass said, his lips barely moving. "His name is really Edward."

"Figures," Jules muttered.

I had no idea how it figured, but whatever. It wasn't like he wasn't going by a nickname too, technically.

"So, Jules, what brings you to Angel's Rest?" His presence was clearly due to more than the empty bowl in front of him. I wondered if his dinner was anyone I knew, but of course I kept that thought to myself. This guy looked like someone who would report Harlow to the health department.

"Augustus was his brother too," Cass said softly.

Jules and I immediately had something in common. We were both looking sharply at his younger brother.

"What is this about Auggie?" Jules demanded.

"Yes, please do elaborate," I said, my voice

dangerous. If he'd gone running his mouth off around the city, we could all be in very big trouble. Specifically Cass and his brother. They could end up tomorrow night's special.

"He can help," Cass insisted.

I rubbed the sides of my nose, where the vagus nerve was, trying to relieve the rapidly building tension. This conversation was using up my spoons. Once I ran out of those, all I had left was knives. And my garrote.

"Who's helping?" Archer grabbed the back of the chair beside mine, pulled it out and flopped down.

"Evening, Hardberg," I said.

"Hardwick," he corrected firmly.

I responded with a barely audible grunt. "What are the statistics on the amount of people who can effectively keep a secret? I was thinking it was four. Cass here seems to think it's five."

"I don't think anyone's done research on that," Archer said, taking in both brothers. "But I saw a meme the other day that said three people can keep a secret if you get rid of two of them."

Jules was staring at the rest of us, his head slowly swiveling back and forth.

"You're all out of your fucking minds. Cassius, who are these nut jobs?" He looked ready to stand up and storm out, which was fine by me as long as he paid for his meal. And left a hefty tip.

"I'll explain everything when Harlow is here," Cass said, his cheeks suddenly pink.

I still wasn't sure we shouldn't keep him out of this. His reaction to those photos said everything we needed to know about his ability to deal with what was to come. The last thing we needed was for him to pass out in the middle of everything. He could put all of us at risk. Especially himself.

Come to think of it, especially me and Harlow too, which I strenuously objected to.

"The chef? What does she have to do with this?" Jules looked so confused, his expression was almost funny. If we were talking about anything but what we were actually skirting around, I'd have a good laugh.

Instead, I scanned the room, watching the last of the customers file out the door, talking and laughing.

Harlow's staff hurried around, picking up the last of the dishes and carrying them to the kitchen. Also talking and laughing.

This place of Harlow's, it was a pocket of warm and cozy in an otherwise dark world. Yeah, I know, so poetic. Accurate though, amiright? Of course I am.

"The truth is," I drawled, "we're gathered here tonight to talk about baking club. Now the first rule of baking club," I held up my finger, "is that we don't talk about baking club."

Archer snorted a laugh and Cass smiled.

Jules looked as confused and irritated as ever. "Baking club? What the fuck are you baking? Weed brownies? Looks to me like you've had too many of them."

"And you haven't had enough," I told him. "If you had, you'd be much more zen. Like my friend Hardcore here." I placed a hand on Archer's shoulder. "He's not easily excited." At least, not as far as I'd seen.

"Hardwick," Archer corrected. "I'm not, but it's not because of weed. I haven't smoked any of that in weeks."

Jules shook his head. "I'm not baking. Whatever the hell is going on here, I don't want anything to do with it." He placed his hands on the table, to either side of his empty bowl, and started to push himself to his feet.

Cass' hand snapped out and grabbed his wrist. "You're going to want to hear this. Sit down."

I think I speak for everyone at the table when I say we were all surprised at his tone. And a little bit aroused.

Even more surprised when Jules actually sat.

"Better be worth it," he muttered.

"Good night," Harlow said as she ushered her staff out the door before closing and locking it behind them. She leaned against it for a moment, her eyes closed, breathing out through plush, pursed lips. Lips that I was now imagining wrapped around my cock. That really would make for a good night.

She shoved herself off the door and walked towards us, taking the last seat at the table. Giving Jules a look like she wished he'd evaporate into thin air.

What do you know, we had something else in common.

"Jules should know what's going on," Cass said, his tone between the commanding one he'd used with his brother, and his normal geek voice. He wanted to be heard, but wasn't convinced we wouldn't dismiss the idea out of hand. Or that Jules wouldn't.

"Can we trust him?" I leaned back and placed my hands behind my head, eyebrow raised.

"I trust him," Cass said. "He knows what happened to Auggie and who did it."

Jules' eyes looked ready to burst out of his face. Which would be fascinating, but unfortunately didn't happen.

Next time, maybe.

"What does this have to do with Gr—" Jules closed his mouth with a snap of his teeth.

"Granger Fairfield," Cass finished for him. "You said you wanted to kill him."

I glanced over to Archer.

He sighed. "There's also no research on how many people say they want to kill someone but don't actually act on it. I'm going to say a high number."

I nodded and turned back to the rest of them.

"Right," Jules said carefully. "It was hypothetical."

"Like people laughing their heads off," I offered. "As far as I know, that's never literally happened."

"Yeah, what Bonehead said." Jules shrugged.

I chuckled. "Bonehead, that's a good one." Although, it fit him better than it fit me. Clearly he was projecting.

Jules smirked, then his expression changed as his brain caught up.

"You're being literal. About Granger Fairfield. You really think you can kill someone like him?"

I'm good at reading people, but I couldn't tell if he was hopeful, or still thought we were out of our minds. Under the circumstances, it might be safe to guess he was hovering right about the middle. He wanted the asshole dead as much as we did, but the average person didn't get together to plan a murder with other people. Not that I know of anyway.

Hey, if there's actually an Evening Murder Club, hook me up, because I'm there.

But I digress.

"We don't just think we can, we know we can," I said. "The question is, do you have the balls to help?" In my experience, casting aspersions on the size of a man's testicles was a very good way to get him to throw his hat into the proverbial ring. We all liked to prove we were blessed with nuts the size of the average-sized moon.

Of course, any bigger than that would be silly.

"He can help," Cass said. "Jules has skills."

I caught the expression on Harlow's face. She was torn between wanting to give Cass what he wanted and kicking Jules' ass out the door.

Totally relatable vibes. I was feeling them myself.

"What sort of skills?" Archer asked.

"Whoa, hold on a minute." Jules raised his hands in front of him, palms out. "Who says I want anything to do with this? You're talking about..." He lowered his voice and whispered, "Killing someone. This is insanity. I'm getting the fuck out of here. Following you to this city was insane enough, but this..."

He pushed himself to his feet and stalked over to the door. Placed his hand on the handle and tried to wrench it open.

The door, being locked, didn't move.

"I can break this fucking door down, or you can unlock it," Jules snarled.

"If we let him leave—" Harlow started.

"He won't say anything," Cass said, his eyes intent on his brother. Staring at him through one eye, since the other was covered with unruly hair.

I have to say, Titmus the Younger was starting to grow on me. That bossy tone was threatening to make my cock grow.

Harlow sighed and stood, pulling her keys out of her pocket and stepping over to unlock the door. "Cass better be right about you," she said darkly. "If you say anything about this to anyone…"

He leaned so his face was right up in hers. "You'll do what, sweetheart? You gonna kill me too?"

She didn't flinch. She met him angry gaze for angry gaze.

"Not at first," she said. "Maybe after a day or two. Maybe three or four. By the end, you'll regret every breath you ever took and every word you ever said."

He looked like he wanted to wrap his hands around her throat and strangle her. The tent in his pants spoke another story. One that was remarkably similar to mine.

She was so fucking hot when she was threatening people. I'd have to work a bit harder to piss her off now and again so she could threaten me like that. Right when she was riding me would be perfect. I'd come then and there.

"You're out of your fucking mind, sweetheart," Jules growled. "You need to get some help."

She stepped away from him and turned to smile at the rest of us, still sitting nicely around the table.

"I already have all the help I need," she said. "Now get the fuck out of my restaurant unless you have something useful to add." Like the meat for tomorrow's lasagna.

I had a feeling he'd be chewy as hell and probably bitter. Someone like him would leave a bad taste in anyone's mouth.

He gave her a last, long look before stepping out into the night and striding past the window and down the street. His footsteps hard on the sidewalk. Punctuating his departure.

She firmly closed the door behind him and locked it again. Shame it didn't hit him on the way out.

"Now," she slipped her keys back into her pocket and returned to her chair. "Where were we?"

CHAPTER 21

HARLOW

"'m sorry about him," Cass said. He shoved his hair back off his face and sank down lower in his seat. "He has anger issues. Anything to do with what happened to Auggie, he... He loses his shit."

"He's not your fault," I assured him, while resisting the urge to agree. That his brother had anger issues was abundantly clear. I sympathized with them both for what their brother went through. It was hellish, to say the least. Jules' problems, though? They went deeper than that. Some people were just assholes.

"Have you met Archer Hardwick?" I made the introductions, somewhat belatedly.

"From what I saw on the news, Wolfgang Taylor-

Francis was murdered," Boner said. "Was that you and Hardball?"

"Hardwick," Archer corrected.

"It might have been," I said cagily.

"What did he do?" Cass asked. That seemed to bother him more than me and Archer potentially killing someone. That darkness I saw in him was becoming more and more evident. The need for control. The desire for vengeance, violence.

Some might say he was unravelling, but I'd compare it to a flower opening, embracing the full extent of their beauty.

"He was abusing his wife," Archer said bluntly, expressionless. Stating facts without giving them emotion. "He did the same to his former wife. And… others. He grew up with violence, like many abusers do. It stops with him."

"It's a good thing he's dead then," Cass said, clearly trying to convince himself as he said each word. By the time he got to the end of the sentence, he was almost as all in as the rest of us.

Boner looked at me questioningly, but he didn't ask. Lucky for him and me. Secrets of the kitchen needed to stay in the kitchen. Not to mention I wasn't ready to tell Cass what he'd eaten the other night. That wasn't a topic for casual conversation.

"It's a very good thing," Boner said instead. "Shame I missed it."

"We missed you while we were doing it," I said, leaning over to pat his hand.

Archer gave me a look that suggested he didn't miss Boner, but he didn't say anything. He was probably trying to think how to make this into a meme.

"So, Granger Fairfield," I said. "We know when he's going to be in the city. What else do we know?"

We spent the next hour planning as best we could, discussing variables and what roles we'd play. Once we'd exhausted everything any of us could think of, I headed into the kitchen to make coffee.

Cass followed me in to help. "I really am sorry about Jules. I was hoping some closure might loosen him up. He blames himself for what happened to our brother. He thinks he should have known and been able to stop it."

"He does, or you do?" I asked gently.

I pulled out cups and placed them under the spout of the coffee machine. Adjusted the settings and pressed the button to start dribbling out hot coffee.

Cass aside. "Both." He took my elbow and turned me around, pressing my back against the counter. "What you're doing, it means a lot. If Auggie was here, he'd want to help. He was always standing up for people who couldn't stand up for themselves."

"He sounded like a good guy," I said.

"He was." Cass leaned in and slanted his mouth over mine. He kissed me lightly, then deepened the kiss as I wound my arms around his neck. He tasted of garlic, tomatoes and a hint of basil. Fresh and delicious, if I said so myself.

He slid his hands down my sides and cupped my ass, before picking me up and placing me on the counter.

"I'm going to eat you, right here," he said, soft but firm.

For a moment, my mind went in a completely different direction and I was torn between laughing and worrying he was being literal. But then he was sliding his hands up my skirt and over the gusset of my panties.

"Cass," I whispered.

Boner and Archer would wonder what we were doing in here.

I barely finished that thought when both of them appeared at the doorway.

"We thought we'd help with the coffee," Boner said. "Don't let us interrupt." He crossed his arms and leaned against the door frame.

Archer swallowed visibly, but did the same on the other side of the door frame.

"You want to watch?" Cass asked as he slid his fingers under the lace of my panties.

"You don't mind?" I asked, directing the question at all three of them.

"I said I'm good with sharing," Boner said. "It doesn't seem like Hard-on minds."

"Hardwick," Archer said absently. "No, I don't mind. Polyamorous lifestyles are becoming more accepted these days." Of course he'd have a statistical study in mind, even at a time like this.

"I want them to watch." Cass' tone was clear. Watching was okay, but that was all. He placed a hand on my chest to lean me back a little further, before tugging my panties down my legs and letting them drop to the floor.

"Let them see," he insisted. "Open your legs and let them look at your pussy. Let them see how wet you are for me."

I gave him a quick glance before parting my thighs, letting the cooler air hit my drenched pussy.

"Just like that." He ran his thumb down my seam before pressing it inside me, all the way to his knuckle. "You like that, don't you?"

"Yes," I whispered. "I need more."

With his other hand, he grabbed a fistful of my

hair and pulled my face closer. "You'll get more when I say you can have more."

"Geek in the streets, freak in the sheets," Boner said to Archer.

Archer murmured his agreement, keeping his eyes on my pussy. He dropped his hand to the front of his pants and squeezed his cock through the fabric.

I was even wetter now. My body aching and begging for much more.

Cass dropped down in front of me, his hands on my thighs. He breathed in deeply, inhaling the scent of me before devouring me with his lips and tongue.

I arched my back and tipped my chin toward the ceiling. His mouth felt amazing. Firm. Commanding. He drove me hard, right to the edge.

Right before I came, he drew his face back. "Take off your top."

Without hesitation, I grabbed the hem and pulled it up and over my head, before tossing it down beside me on the counter.

"Bra too," Cass ordered. "Show us those gorgeous breasts of yours."

All their eyes on me, I reached back to unhook my bra and let my breasts fall free from the lacy confines.

"So fucking beautiful," Boner said softly. His hand was also on the front of his pants, gripping the rapidly growing bulge there.

"Ten out of ten," Archer agreed.

Boner snorted. "Twenty out of ten, bro."

"That's not possible, but whatever." Archer shrugged, never tearing his gaze from me.

Cass dropped his face back between my legs, running his tongue up and down my seam and grazing my clit with his teeth. "Come for us."

He barely finished speaking when I did as he ordered, coming hard and fast against his mouth. The whole kitchen disappeared, right down to the cool countertop under my heated skin. The only thing I was aware of was the three men, and bliss as it encompassed me.

"Fuck, you come so nicely, love," Boner said. "Definitely twenty out of ten."

Archer didn't correct him this time.

Cass rose to his feet and kissed my mouth, letting me taste myself as he undid his jeans and pushed them and his boxers down his hips. Hands on my thighs, he pulled me to him until his cock was nestled against my entrance.

"Tell me to fuck you," he ordered.

I was still breathless when I said, "Fuck me, please." If I didn't have him inside me right then, I was going to explode.

"Louder," he insisted. "I want those two to know and understand you're mine."

I tipped my head back again. "Fuck. Me."

He gripped my hips and drove himself into me, slow at first, but then with more force. Until he was buried inside me, all the way to the hilt.

"You feel fucking incredible," he whispered. "So fucking tight for me." He stood like that for a minute or two, his eyes closed, savoring the feel of our bodies joined. He pulled out slowly and slammed back in. "Touch yourself. Make those nipples hard for me."

I raised my hands and cupped my breasts, palming my nipples until they were rock hard.

"Good girl," Boner said. He pushed his own pants down and had his cock in his hand. Working it slowly up and down as he watched.

Archer glanced at him for a moment, swallowed deeply, then did the same, pulling out his cock and stroking it. Rubbing his thumb over his tip, spreading pre-cum over his skin.

Cass thrust into me slowly and evenly, trying not to rush but needing to give into his own body. His own needs. His desire to spill himself inside me.

"Touch yourself," he whispered, dipping his chin. "I want you to come around my cock."

I dropped one hand from my breast, down to my clit, rubbing my fingers around it, spreading my juices and pushing myself back to the precipice of a second orgasm.

"Come for me," Cass insisted. "Right. Now."

I couldn't hold back. I came again, my muscles clenching around his cock and forcing an orgasm out of him. He drove into me over and over, milking himself for every drop, while filling me with his release.

We both slumped down together, panting lightly and trying to catch our breath.

"Harlow, you're incredible," he whispered.

"No, you are, Cassius," I told him. "That was so good."

Better than good. I never knew I enjoyed being watched so much. I felt beautiful. Powerful. Desirable. Like a goddess.

"You need a new item on your menu," Boner said. "Cream pie." He grimaced as he came, a string of cum shooting from his tip, over his hand and onto the floor.

Archer snorted and followed suit, keeping his cum contained in his hand as he ground against it.

"I've never enjoyed being a wanker more," Boner said with a grin.

"Speak for yourself." Archer headed over to the sink to wash his hands before drying them and tucking his cock back in his pants.

"Good try, but you're just as big a wanker as I am right now," Boner teased.

Cass made a face and slid out of me. "Thank you. For letting me fuck you and for letting me be me." That meant everything to him, it shone in his eyes.

Here, with us, he could be himself without any of us judging him. Without us wanting him to hold back. If fucking me, ordering me around, and being watched were his things, we should absolutely do it more often.

I cupped his face with my hands. "I wouldn't want you to be anyone else." Boner was right, he was a geek in the streets and a freak in the sheets. You better believe I was here for all of it. I kissed his mouth, the taste of me lingering on his lips.

He wrapped his arms around me and pressed his cheek to mine. Softly he said something that sounded like, "I could fall for you."

I didn't say anything back, but the truth was I could fall for him too. Honestly, I could fall for all of them.

If we could survive dealing with Granger Fairfield without getting caught or killed.

CHAPTER 22
HARLOW

"I s it time yet?" Boner whispered.

I checked my watch, the analogue kind that didn't illuminate. The hands were almost where we needed them to be.

"Soon," I whispered back. I wiped my palms on my jeans and peered across the street.

The brownstone in West Village was exactly the kind of place I'd buy if I didn't mind drawing attention to myself. It screamed money, power, influence. If I looked for longer, corruption and depravity.

Everything I despised. A beautiful building like this was wasted on someone like Fairfield.

Beside me, Boner shifted, brushing his arm against mine a couple of times.

"Sorry, itchy left nut. They always get itchy when I'm nervous."

I snorted softly. "We all have our quirks."

"Oh? What's yours?" He peered past me before drawing his head back. "You look as cool as a cucumber sandwich."

"Do people really eat those?" Give me a good old-fashioned PB and J any day.

He made a disgusted sound at the back of his throat. "Not me, love. Too fancy for my taste."

"Are you saying you're not fancy?" I teased.

"Fuck no," he said with a short laugh. "Just not cucumber sandwich fancy. Give me a good steak any day. Or some steak and kidney pie."

"I'll keep that in mind," I said.

Granger Fairfield wouldn't be needing his kidneys for much longer, but I wouldn't feed them to Boner unless he pissed me off. Which is to say, my options were open, but it was unlikely.

He cleared his throat. He must have had an inkling what I was thinking, but wouldn't say it with Cass listening in.

I chuckled to myself.

"Are you ready?" Cass said in my ear. "Fairfield is about to arrive."

Just as he said that, a dark town car slid around the corner and headed for the spot in front of the brownstone. The back door opened and Granger

Fairfield stepped out one door, his security out the other.

"My replacement should be here shortly," the security guy was saying. "Denton is sick, so they sent in a new guy."

Fairfield seemed disinterested. He grabbed a bag out of the back of the car and carried it up to the stoop.

Expressionless, the security guy followed him up the steps and inside.

"We could have taken him out here," Boner complained.

"There's at least six security cameras in the vicinity," Cass said. "Someone would be suspicious if they all went down at the same time."

The town car slid away, replaced by a black SUV. A car you wouldn't pay much attention to on a normal night. One that blended in with the area. I wouldn't have looked twice if I didn't know what I was looking for. Namely Archer stepping out of the car and up to the front of the brownstone.

He wore a dark suit that looked tailor-made, and a crisp white shirt. Very different from his usual jeans and T-shirts, he looked good enough to peel off all the layers of fabric and eat him up. How would he feel about a bit of role-play involving that suit?

Maybe with me and a pencil skirt and heels. Throw in a desk and we had a fantasy on our hands.

Heat burned through my blood and down to my core, threatening to drench my panties.

Later, I told myself. I couldn't get distracted right now. Just as well Boner wasn't wearing a suit too, or I would have been in serious trouble.

I blinked a couple of times to clear my thoughts and watch Archer striding toward the brownstone, his hands in his jacket pockets.

He knocked on the door and stood with his arms crossed, waiting for it open before stepping inside.

"Almost party time," Boner whispered. "I have to say, getting him in there was a stroke of genius."

"Thank you," Cass said, sounding like he was blushing. It was his idea; he'd hacked the security firm to have Archer added to the roster. Along with a resume that made him a shoe-in for filling in when the regular security was sick. And by sick, I mean recovering from an unfortunate dose of food poisoning. He'd be fine in a couple of days.

My competitor he ordered the food from? They were looking into it. Since they tried to steal my recipe for sweet potato ravioli, I didn't feel too bad about it.

The door opened again and the security guy

stepped out, hurrying towards the subway station at the end of the block.

I waited until he was out of sight and nodded. "Let's do this."

Boner grabbed my hand and we rose from the spot between two buildings where we'd crouched for the last half-hour. We stayed in the shadows while a couple walked past, before stepping out and crossing the street.

He tapped on the door and we waited for Archer to swing it open.

"I'm so sorry to bother you," I said in my best apologetic tone. "My boyfriend here is drunk and he insisted he knows the man who lives here."

"I do know him," Boner protested, slurring his words. "Philippo and I went to school together. He's a goddamn motherfucker, but he told me if I was ever here I should look him up. So here I am, in all my fuckin' glory." He spread his arms to either side.

"There's no one named Philippo here," Archer said, glancing at Boner like he thought he was out of his mind. In other words, his usual expression when he looked at the Englishman.

"Of course there is." Boner staggered past Archer. He tipped his head back and shouted, "Phil! Where are you, you bastard? Come out here and say hi to your old friend Rastus!"

Rastus?

I exchanged bemused glances with Archer and offered half a shrug. Boner said he'd get Fairfield's attention, but he hadn't elaborated how. Apparently it worked, because Fairfield trotted down the stairs at the center of the house, staring at Boner.

"What's going on here? Why are these people in my home?" He looked like he'd throw us out onto the street, Archer included. *Especially* Archer, since he was the one who let us in and was still standing beside the door.

The door he closed and stood in front of, his arms crossed.

"Phil, there you are," Boner said, sounding perfectly sober.

"There's no one by that name here," Fairfield said coldly. "Get the hell out."

I smiled. "I don't think so. Archer?"

"There's no one else here," Archer said. "There was a young woman, but I untied her and helped her out the back door. She's on her way somewhere safe." He must have contacted Cass to arrange someone to take her home.

"What the fuck?" Fairfield backed up a step or two. "I paid good money…"

Apparently he realized he was about to incriminate himself, because he slammed his mouth shut, turned and started to run for the back of the building.

Boner and I gave chase, trotting down the hallway a few feet behind.

Fairfield darted into a side room and Boner held out his arm to keep me behind him.

"Prick's going to have a—"

Fairfield stepped back out of the room, a gun in his hand. "Did you think I'd be unprepared?"

"We didn't think you would, but we'd hoped," Boner said. "I mean, guys like you usually rely on other people. It's not often they have the balls to deal with anything themselves."

He was right. There could have been a panic button in the room he just vacated. The cops might be on their way right now. We needed to deal with this quickly.

Fairfield rolled his eyes. "Who are you and what do you want?" He shook his head. "You know what, it doesn't matter." He raised the gun and pointed it at Boner's head. "You shouldn't have tried screwing with me."

"You're absolutely right," Boner said. "We shouldn't have. Our bad. We'll just be leaving now." He took a step back.

"You're not going anywhere," Fairfield growled.

"You're not going to shoot me," Boner said. "If you

do, then how will I learn? This whole lesson was for nothing. You wouldn't want a perfectly good teachable moment to go to waste, would you?"

"What are you talking about?" Fairfield lowered the gun slightly, but raised it again. "You should have learned a long time ago."

"My mom always said I'd get myself in trouble someday, because I always have to see something through, even if it seems like a bad idea at the time. You know the expression, fuck around and find out? I've always enjoyed a bit of fucking around. The finding out part? Not such a big fan. I bet almost anything we have that in common, yeah?"

Boner lowered his hands to his sides. "Consequences are always such a pain in the ass, wouldn't you say? Wait, you wouldn't know. You haven't had to face any yet. It must be nice to have so much money you can buy your way out of anything."

In my earpiece, Cass growled. I mean an actual, full on feral growl. Under any other circumstance, it would have been hot as hell. Right now, he reminded me of what was at stake here. The things Fairfield did. Why Cass wanted to help us in the first place.

"He has connections too," I said. "They've been a big help too, haven't they Fairfield?"

He glanced around Boner at me and frowned. "Have we met?"

I stepped up beside the Englishman. "Not in person. You knew my sister, Lettie St. James."

He shook his head, but I could tell he knew exactly who I was referring to. I could have hoped for a flicker of guilt, but it never came. Of course not. It never would with men like him. Their only regret would be getting caught.

"Enough," Fairfield snapped. His grip on the gun tightened. Coldly, he regarded us both, calculating how fast he'd have to be to kill one, then the other. He aimed the gun back at Boner.

Rude. Did he think he could shoot Boner, then overpower me? Did he believe I'd be too slow? Had he underestimated the rage I'd lived with since my sister's murder?

My guess was yes, yes and also yes.

His finger tightened around the trigger.

I went for my knife.

The door opened behind Fairfield and Archer stepped inside. Before Fairfield could react to his presence, Archer plunged a needle into the side of his neck and squeezing the contents until the syringe was empty.

"What the—"

Boner and I both took the distraction, leaping at Fairfield. Boner to grab his wrist and try to wrench the gun out of his hand. Me to drive a knife into his thigh.

Goddamn it, I was aiming for his groin.

Either way, Boner and Fairfield wrestled for the gun for a few moments before Boner grabbed it and tossed it back over his shoulder. It clattered on the hardwood and slid almost to the front door.

I pulled out my knife, ready to try again, when Fairfield's eyes rolled back in his head and he started to fall. Both of the guys grabbed him before he could hit the floor. Hefting him up between them like he was now the drunk one, they carried him out the back of the house and around the front.

"We need to get him into the car," Archer said.

I hurried to open the back of the SUV so the guys could toss him inside like a sack of potatoes. Actually, they'd probably be gentler with potatoes.

Archer slammed the hatch closed and hurried around to the driver's side door. "Let's get out of here."

"Now the party really begins." Boner grinned and slid into the back seat, leaving me to claim shotgun.

"My favorite part," I said, clicking my seatbelt in as Archer peeled the car away from the side of the road.

CHAPTER 23

HARLOW

"He's waking up." Cass stood beside the table, looking down at Fairfield, who was bound to it, hands and feet.

"You don't have to watch any of this." I walked over to him and placed my arm around him, resting my head on his shoulder. "If you need to leave, no one is going to blame you."

"I'll blame me," he said. "After what he did to my brother, I owe it to Augustus to stay."

"He'd understand if you didn't," I assured him. "The things you're going to see, you won't be able to unsee them."

"What about you?" He wrapped his arm around me. "You won't be able to unsee it either."

"I've never been bothered by raw meat," I said simply.

"She seemed to enjoy your raw meat." Boner stepped to the other side of me and grinned. "And mine that night she and I shared."

I snorted a soft laugh. "See, I'm a big fan of raw meat. I can stomach just about anything. If it gets too much, the toilet is over there." I gestured off to the right.

Fairfield groaned, drawing our attention to him. Sluggishly, his eyes opened. Widened. He tried to call out, but the gag in his mouth muffled his words.

"At least he hasn't pissed himself yet," Boner said.

"Yet," I agreed.

"I have a few tools you can use." Archer entered the room, carrying a case. He set it down beside Fairfield and opened it.

"I think I just got an erection," Boner said. "Hardware, my dude, you're my new hero."

"Hardwick," Archer said like he might use one of the implements on Boner.

Ignoring them both, I stepped over to take a look.

"Very nice." He'd included several knives, a pair of scissors, pinking shears, a couple of pieces of rough rope, two pairs of pliers, a spatula, several different sized vegetable peelers and an apple corer.

"A spatula?" Cass asked over my shoulder.

"I can demonstrate it for you if you like?" Boner

reached for it, pulling it out of the case and bran-dishing it in front of Cass' face.

Cass swatted it away. "But what is it really for?"

"Scooping up guts," Archer said, his expression deadpan. "It's easier than bare hands."

"I shouldn't have asked," Cass groaned. But then he added, "And the apple corer?"

"Anal." Once again, Archer's face was expressionless.

"I don't want you to demonstrate," Cass said to Boner before the Englishman could say a word.

Boner grinned. "Anal is better with my cock. I am happy to demonstrate that for you any time." He patted Cass on the shoulder. "Now, where do we start with this prick?" He and Archer looked at me and Cass. For Cass and me, this was personal. For them, it was a bit of fun.

I thought for a moment before picking up a pair of scissors and stepping around the table. Grabbing one of Fairfield's fingers, I snipped it off slowly, working the blades through muscle and bone, and tossed it beside his face.

"How many women have you touched with those fingers?" I worked off another. "How many young men?"

While he moaned in pain, I removed all of the fingers from one hand, letting him bleed on the table.

"Cass, would you like to do the honors?" I nodded toward Fairfield's intact hand.

Cass was looking a little green as he shook his head, then nodded. "I don't know."

Fairfield turned his face toward him, pleading through the gag. It seemed he'd decided, if any one of us would give him mercy, it would be Cass.

"You could always start with a toe," Boner suggested. "Toes are easier."

I offered Cass the scissors.

His hand shaking, he took them and slid his fingers into the ring handles. Tentatively, he took Fairfield's pinky finger between his thumb and fore-finger and brought the blades of the scissors down to the webbing. He closed his eyes and winced as he squeezed the scissors, slowly slicing through until the finger fell away. It landed on the table, rolled once and lay still.

Fairfield screamed and sobbed, writhing and trying to get away from Cass.

Cass opened his eyes and stared down at the dismembered digit. He handed me back the scissors, turned and ran toward the toilet to empty his stomach.

"You did really well," I called out to him.

"Huh, that was surgical precision," Boner said

admiringly. "Can I have a turn?" He held his hand out for the scissors.

"Of course." I lay them across his palm and stood back to watch him remove the rest of Fairfield's fingers.

"You're hot when you're dismembering people," Archer said, whispering in my ear.

I flashed him a grin. "I had the right tools. I need a place like this." I looked around me. We stood in a converted apartment with a view out to an otherwise unassuming neighborhood. The floors were concrete, the walls brick. All immaculately clean except the blood on the table. Which was starting to pool and threatening to drip off onto the floor.

"You're welcome to use it anytime," he said. "If you have to bring anyone here, my door is open."

"I appreciate that." I leaned over to kiss his cheek.

"I have to admit," Boner said as he moved over to start on Fairfield's toes, "I visualized Vigilante University, but it never looked like this. It always looked a bit more like…" Snip. "A university campus." Snip. "With lecture theaters." Snip. "And rooms for tutorials and shit like that." Snip. "And a univiersity bar." Snip.

"It pays to have an open mind," Archer said. He gave me a look and mouthed, "Vigilante University?"

I shrugged one shoulder. "It sounds better than Felon University."

Boner looked over and grinned. "I'd love to attend FU." He frowned for a moment. "I'm trying to think of a way to add C and K to that."

"Of course you are," I told him. "Except I don't see us as felons anyway."

"Avenging Angel University?" Archer suggested.

"Asshole Torturers R-Us," Boner said with a grin. He snipped off the last toe and set the scissors aside. "Now I really don't like this guy."

"Because you're lack toes intolerant?" Archer deadpanned.

Boner stared at him for a moment before he burst out laughing. "That's fucking hilarious, my dude. Also, I've finally figured out what fingerless gloves are for. Or should I say, who."

I shook my head at them both.

"What's up, love?" Boner cocked his head at me. "You know the sharpest thing in this place is my wit." He waggled his eyebrows.

"Keep telling yourself that," I said. I turned my face as Cass stepped back into the room, looking pale. "Are you okay?" I slipped my hand into his and drew him to my side. He wasn't trembling anymore, his body warm and firm against mine. Comforting me when I was trying to comfort him.

He nodded slowly. "Much better now." Reluctantly, he looked over to Fairfield. "I know I have to remind myself what he did to my brother, but..."

"He did the same thing to my sister," I said calmly. I was in no way going to feel sorry for Granger Fairfield. Not for a second. Did we *need* to do these things to him?

Absolutely.

It was a small punishment in comparison to the evil he'd done. Why shouldn't he suffer when the people we loved had suffered? None of it would take away the hurt, but it would make us feel better for a while.

"And lots of other people's brothers and sisters," Archer said. "He's getting exactly what he deserves."

"What he said," Boner agreed. "Now, which one of you is going to slice off his cock?"

Fairfield was getting weaker as he lost more and more blood, but he thrashed against his bindings at that. Struggling to get away, although he must have known he couldn't. Even if he wasn't outnumbered, he'd find it almost impossible to walk without toes.

"I'm not touching his dick," I said, disgusted at the thought. It wasn't much bigger than his pinky finger, but...yuck.

"I'm sorry, but I'm out," Cass said. He looked just

as disgusted. If he went anywhere near that thing, he might be sick again.

"You hear that?" Boner patted Fairfield's bicep. "No one wants to touch your willy."

Fairfield stared back at him balefully. Did he think he was getting out of here otherwise intact?

"It might be time for the bath," Archer said.

"You want to clean this guy?" Boner jerked his thumb toward Fairfield. "We've barely started making a mess with him."

"Not in water," Archer said evenly. As if that explained everything.

Boner stared at him for a moment before understanding dawned. "Not hot water either? Let me guess, soda?" He clearly didn't think soda was involved.

"Vinegar and bicarb soda?" He didn't believe that either, although he seemed to like the idea. It would certainly be dramatic. A human volcano, but without the fun of lava.

"Hydrofluoric acid," Archer said. "It'll break down bone and tissue slowly, making it hurt, but easy to clean up afterwards."

Boner stepped over to him, placed his hands to either side of his head and loudly kissed him on the mouth. "You, my friend are bloody awesome."

Archer blinked at him a couple of times before

gesturing toward Fairfield. "I could use a hand carrying him there."

"Anything for you." Boner stepped around to Fairfield's feet and started to remove the straps from the table. His ankles were still tightly bound together, as were his wrists.

After a moment, Cass stepped over to help them. The three of them carried Fairfield to the bathroom and pushed him into the bath. He slid down the side and landed in the bottom with a thud and a cry of pain.

They reattached the restraints to rings screwed into the side of the porcelain and stood back.

At one end of the bath a drum was connected to a tap, not unlike my box at home. When Archer leaned over to open the tap, acid started to trickle out slowly. At first, it didn't seem to do anything, then Fairfield started to whimper.

With the plug firmly in place, the bath filled slowly, liquid gradually creeping up over his legs, then his stomach.

I half expected to hear it sizzle, but of course it didn't. It wasn't a pan full of hot oil. This time.

"That should do it for now." Archer turned the tap, cutting off the flow. "We don't want him to drown in there."

"Yet," Boner and I said in unison.

"Yes, yet," Archer agreed. "He can have some fun in there for a while first."

"I don't know, but I think it's us having the fun," Boner said. "I know I am. All this revenge is making me horny." He adjusted the front of his pants.

Fairfield stared up at us with wide, terrified eyes. As the acid went to work on his skin, he finally understood. He wasn't getting out of this alive. His only hope now was to die quickly. That wish wasn't going to come true either.

I startled as Cass' phone rang.

He pulled it out of his pocket and glanced at the screen. "It's Jules." He answered the call and pressed the phone to his ear. "Hey, what's going—" He stopped to listen. "He is? Isn't that, um…" He looked down at Fairfield and frowned. "It's too bad. His family must be worried."

He listened again. "What makes you think I know where he is?"

Jules raised his voice, loud enough for me to hear him, if not what he was saying.

Cass winced. "All right, fine. Give me a minute." He lowered the phone. "Jules had a change of heart…"

CHAPTER 24

HARLOW

"This is awkward." I stood between Boner and Archer, watching Cass and Jules look down at Fairfield.

"It's dangerous," Boner said. "What guaranteed do we have we can trust this asshat?"

"I don't think he'd betray his brother," I said.

Archer pulled out his phone and took a photo of them. "Right now he's an accessory. He'd be throwing himself under the bus too." Instead of putting his phone away, started scrolling through his social media feed like we weren't standing in a bathroom with a man being slowly deconstructed by acid.

"This is the fuck who destroyed our brother," Jules said, his voice devoid of expression.

"This is him." Cass put a hand on his older brother's shoulder. "Not for much longer."

"I can't decide if this is as messed up as shit or…" Jules shook his head.

Boner smirked. "Of course it's as messed up as shit. So was he." He pointed a beringed finger at Fairfield.

"You think he would have hesitated to do the same thing to you? To Harlow? It's only luck that what happened was to your siblings and not to you."

Jules looked at me like he couldn't have cared less if it was me. That if he could swap me with his youngest brother, he'd strongly consider it.

Honestly, I'd do the same, but I'd never wish what happened to Lettie on anyone else except the people who did it to her. They deserved to be covered in honey and tied out in the hot sun, beside an ant hill so the ants could slowly peel off their skin, then feast on their internal organs.

"This is still fucked up," he muttered.

"How did you know he was missing?" I asked.

His lips thinned, jaw squared. For a moment I thought he wasn't going to answer.

Only when Cass turned to him questioningly, he said, "I went over there to take care of him myself. Saw the gun on the floor. The doors were unlocked. Figured you got to him before I did."

"You figured right." Boner looked suitably smug.

Jules smirked at him. "You forgot something." He

pulled a phone out of the back pocket of his faded black jeans.

"I've got mine," Boner said, tapping his own pocket.

"It's not yours, dickhead." Jules rolled his eyes. "This belongs to him." He pointed the phone toward Fairfield. "It was lying on the floor near the back door."

I winced. "We must have missed it." No doubt it fell out when the men were carrying him out of the brownstone. I wondered why he didn't have one on him, but not everyone was attached to their phones twenty-four seven. He could just as easily have put it aside somewhere and we didn't see where. We'd been too busy trying to leave before the cops came, to look for it.

If Jules was able to walk through the place, I guess Fairfield hadn't called them after all. That figured. We could have taken our time.

"No shit," Jules said with a derisive snort. "This could have all sorts of incriminating information on it."

Judging by the way Fairfield stared at him, his eyes wider than ever, he wasn't wrong. He couldn't be worried about what they'd do to him for letting us get our hands on their information, could they? What could they do to him that we weren't already doing?

The fact he was so scared spoke volumes about how powerful these men were. How dangerous.

My heart skipped. That phone might contain the details of the last three men I was hunting. One quick look and I could know their names. That was all I needed to track them down and end them.

"Have you looked at it?" Cass asked, eyeing the device like it was a gold nugget.

"It's locked," Jules said. He hesitated for a moment before handing it to his brother.

Cass tapped at the screen, swallowed hard and glanced up at me. "It needs…a thumbprint." He looked nauseous again.

To be honest, I was relieved. A thumbprint was easier than a passcode or facial recognition. Trying to figure out the passcode could take forever, and we'd have to remove the gag from Fairfield to use his face. He'd scream or cry the moment we did. Perhaps plead for his life. We couldn't risk the neighbors hearing.

Boner grinned. "That won't be a problem. We happen to have a couple of spare thumbs lying around." As if that was an everyday occurrence for regular people. Thumbs scattered throughout the house like phone chargers, or tissue boxes.

"I can do it if you want," I offered. If the idea of handling dismembered digits was too much for Cass, it wasn't for me. Besides, I really wanted a look at what was on that phone.

"I…" Cass took in a deep breath and let it out with the words, "I can do it."

"Cassius—" Jules started.

"I can do this," Cass said again, more firmly this time. "Harlow, you might want to see what's on here." Without another word, he turned and headed out to the other room.

I gave Jules a quick glance before following Cass over to the table.

"Lucky thumbs are shorter than the other fingers," I said. "It makes it easier to find them." It didn't hurt that Boner lined them up in order, with the middle fingers sitting across the pointers as though Fairfield crossed his fingers for luck. It hadn't worked too well for him, maybe it would work better for us.

"Right." Cass pinched the right thumb, grimacing as he picked it up and pressed the pad against the phone. "I guess it's the other one." He picked up the left thumb and tried again. The screen opened onto a generic screensaver that came with the phone.

"It figures he'd be unimaginative," I said. Of course, he wouldn't put anything incriminating on the lock screen or the home screen. If anyone saw, he would have gotten into trouble long before now. It also figured that the phone was almost fully charged. Fairfield was chaotic evil at best.

"I'll change it so we can get in with a passcode," Cass said, tapping on the settings icon. He changed it to one one three seven. "We won't forget that."

"No, we won't," I agreed. It was the street number for my restaurant. I was surprised he noticed or remembered. The fact he did was touching. "Can we have a look at his contacts?"

"Yeah." Careful not to touch the photos icon, Cass brought up Fairfield's contacts and held the screen so we could both look.

"He knew some very rich, influential people," I said. I knew that already, but some of these names were surprising. Honestly, many would surprise the entire world.

Some were likely to be innocent business contacts, with absolutely no knowledge of Fairfield's activities. Others though... If we could prove they were involved, they were going to end the same way.

I wasn't surprised Fairfield knew Reuben Brantley. From what I heard, he was a notorious mob boss from Australia. I suspected he was one of the ones who didn't know what Fairfield was up to. His interests lay elsewhere. Hopefully he wouldn't decide to track us down and retaliate. The last thing I needed was a mob boss taking a hit out on me.

Although, he'd have to find me first.

"And a few pseudonyms." Cass pointed to someone referred to as Eros, and another who went by Hypnos. Right at the bottom of the list was Zeus.

"Coincidence?" I asked, not believing that for a moment. Three men, three Greek gods.

These were the last three men who murdered my sister. I was certain of it.

"I'll send the information to your phone." One by one, he sent the details to me, making my phone vibrate in my pocket. "It'll take a while to do the rest of them. I'll look into them and see if they need to be…"

"Dealt with?" I offered.

He swallowed. "Yeah, dealt with."

I put a hand on his bicep. "You don't have to take part in any of this. You and your brother, you could both walk out of here right now and not look back."

I'd be disappointed if I never saw Cass again, but Jules could get lost and I wouldn't lose any sleep.

"I'm staying," Cass said firmly. "I'm in this with you until the end. Whatever that may be."

I nodded slowly and squeezed his arm. "I'm glad you are. What about Jules? Do you think seeing Fairfield like that has given him what he needs?"

"What's that?" Jules asked from the doorway. "What do I need?"

"Closure," Cass said softly. "We can finally put Auggie to rest. Get on with our lives."

"Is that what you're doing, Cassius?" Jules stalked into the room. "Getting on with your life? Is that what this is?" He waved a hand toward the table containing ten dismembered fingers and ten dismembered toes. Not to mention a shit ton of blood.

"That's exactly what this is," Cass said. "I'm doing something meaningful."

Jules stared at him. "You're doing something twisted. Not to mention illegal."

"Like I said, you can walk out the door and never look back," I told him coldly. "You saw what you came to see."

I hadn't missed it when he said he tried to take care of Fairfield himself. What form would that have taken? I couldn't see evidence of a gun on him. Or a knife, for that matter. What was he planning to do, yell Fairfield to death? Perhaps glare at him until his heart stopped?

"Have I?" Jules looked at me sideways, dark eyes intense. "Do you seriously think seeing that asshole like that is going to make me feel better about what he did to our brother?" He gestured back towards the bathroom with his whole arm.

"No, because it doesn't take away the pain of

what he did to my sister." I tried to keep my voice even, although my emotions threatened to spill over.

"All it does is make me feel better that he can't do it again. That lasts for a couple of days before I'm reminded he's only one person. There's so many more like him."

Jules dropped his hand to his side with a slap. He pressed his lips together and half closed his eyes.

"Exactly," he said, his voice gravelly with his own barely contained emotion. "That sack of shit dying isn't gonna bring Augustus back. It's not going to erase what I saw when I walked into his room and found him…" He screwed his eyes shut.

"Jules." Cass walked over and put his arms around his older brother. Jules stiffened for a moment before returning the embrace.

"It's so fucking fucked up," Jules whispered.

"It's extremely fucked up," I agreed. "I wish I got to him before he got to your brother. Then it wouldn't have happened at all."

Jules all but shoved Cass away. "You were looking for him?"

"For years," I said.

"You could have stopped this." His tone was all accusation.

"Julius—" Cass started.

Jules shook his head. "No. If she had found him, Augustus would be here right now."

"What Fairfield did wasn't her fault," Cass insisted. "You know that."

"Do I?" Jules rounded on him. His jaw set, he turned and stalked out the door, slamming it shut behind him.

"I'm sorry about him," Cass said softly. "He didn't mean it. He knows there's nothing you could have done." He didn't seem so sure.

Maybe I was projecting my thoughts on to him, because I blamed myself. If I spent less time setting up my restaurant and more time hunting these monsters, I might have gotten to Fairfield first. I'd split my attention between two things, trying to hold onto some kind of normality. How many people had hurt because I did that?

How many had died?

How many would still die while we tried to figure out who Eros, Hypnos and Zeus were?

We were in a race to find them before they destroyed more lives.

And before they found us.

EPILOGUE
ZEUS

"Boss, it would seem Granger Fairfield is dead," Thomas remarked.

"Of course he is," I said with a grunt. Why did I surround myself with toadies like him? Yes men and their Captain Obvious routine.

I rewound the footage and watched it again.

Fairfield stood inside his own property, the one he used when he visited New York. In his hand, he held a gun, pointed at two figures covered from head to toe in black. One looked female, but I couldn't be sure. They were speaking, but no sound accompanied the video.

Exactly as it happened the last handful of times I watched it, the back door opened and a man stepped through. The camera only caught a glimpse of his face before he plunged something into Fairfield's neck. Some kind of drug.

More talking, then Fairfield was falling to his knees before they picked him up and carried him out.

Further on in the video, approximately fifteen minutes later, another figure stepped down the corridor, this one also covered in black, a mask over his face. He leaned over to scoop something up off the floor.

Fairfield's phone. That could be problematic, depending on what they were after. This could be related to his other business dealings.

I suspected not.

Whoever they were, they were coming after us.

After *me*.

I rewound the video again, this time stopping on the one, grainy face. I took a screenshot and sent it off to one of my people.

When we found him, we'd find the rest of them. And we would.

I'd get to them before they got to me.

Thank you for reading! The story continues in Heart Rending If you'd love a... heartwarming bonus scene, you can get that here

ABOUT THE AUTHOR

Maggie Alabaster writes reverse harem and, paranormal, sci-fi and fantasy romance.

She lives in NSW, Australia with one spouse, two daughters, one dog, and countless birds.

Jo Bradley writes contemporary romance.

Sign up for Maggie's newsletter! Sign Up!

Join Maggie's reader group! Join here!

Follow Maggie on Bookbub! Click here to follow me!

Check out Maggie's website- www.maggiealabaster.com

ALSO BY MAGGIE ALABASTER

Best Served Cold

Heart Stopping

Heart Rending

Heart Breaking

Heart Beating

Aurora Hollow duet

Take Me Slowly Part 1

Take Me Slowly Part 2

Ruck Boys

Filthy Ruck

Hard Ruck

Twisted Ruck

Bad Ruck

Dirty Ruck

Deadly Ruck

Sparrow and the Mafia Kings

Possessive

Ruined

Corrupted

Pucking Dark Hearts

Pucking Hearts Collide

Pucking Forbidden Hearts

Pucking Hardened Hearts

Dusk Bay Demons

Puck Drop

Breakaway

Power Play

Brutal Academy

Book 1 Heartless

Book 2 Cruel

Book 3 Vengeful

Court of Blood and Binding

Book 1 Song of Scent and Magic

Book 2 Crown of Mist and Heat

Book 3 Sword of Balm and Shadow

Book 4 Whisper of Frost and Flame

Dark Masque

Book 1 Bait

Book 2 Prey

Book 3 Trap

Novella A Very Dark Masque Christmas

Saving Abbie

Book 1 Pitch

Book 2 Pound

Book 3 Session

Book 4 Muse

Book 5 Rhythm

Book 6 Encore

Novella Venomous

Saving Abbie books 1-4

Saving Abbie books 4-6 + Venomous

Ruthless Claws

Book 1 Ivory

Book 2 Crimson

Book 3 Elodie

Harmony's Magic

Book 1 Summoned by Fire

Book 2 Summoned by Fate

Book 3 Summoned by Desire

Shifter's Vault

Book 1 Discarded

Book 2 Deceived

Book 3 Disgraced

My Alien Mates

Book 1 Star Warriors

Book 2 Star Defenders

Book 3 Star Protectors

Academy of Modern Magic

Book 1 Digital Magic

Book 2 Virtual Magic

Book 3 Logical Magic

Complete Collection

Summer's Harem

Book 1: Shimmer

Book 2: Glimmer

Book 3: Flicker

Complete collection

Short reads

Taken by the Snowmen

Jingle All the Way

Also by Maggie Alabaster and Erin Yoshikawa

Caught by the Tide

Book 1–Pursued by Shadows

Book 2 Pursued by Darkness

Book 3 Pursued by Monsters

READING ORDER

This is the recommended reading order of Maggie's contemporary mafia RH.

Sparrow and the Mafia Kings

Saving Abbie

Dark Daze

Dark Masque

Brutal Academy

Dusk Bay Demons

Pucking Dark Hearts

Ruck Boys

A Very Dark Masque Christmas